Winning Love

Harmony Noble

Revised Edition: March 2024

ISBN 979-8-9884714-4-8, 978-1-963074-62-8, 978-1-963074-99-4

Story creation, cover, and illustrations by Melody Noble & Harmony Curtis

Thank you for choosing this book.
We hope the story
brought you as much joy reading it
as we had in creating it!

We'd love to hear from you! Feel free to reach out via email at TrueLoveWriters@gmail.com, and follow us on Instagram, Facebook, TikTok at @truelovewriters for the latest updates and behind-the-scenes fun.

Get access to exclusive offers, bonus content, new release updates, and recommendations for more great reads.

Sign up for our e-newsletter at HarmonyNoble.com.

Dedicated to Joan Noble,

Your unwavering support and encouragement in me, both as a writer and person, extends beyond the confines of family ties. You have been there with kind words of encouragement throughout my creative journey. Thank you for being my biggest cheerleader and an endless source of love!

Winning Love

Harmony Noble

TrueLoveWriters

Chapter 1

Baby's Rocky Start

Win · ning

Dictionary– Definitions from Oxford Languages

/'winiNG/
Adjective

1. gaining, resulting in, or relating to victory in a contest or competition.
   a winning streak
   - Similar: victorious, successful, conquering, triumphant, unbeaten, first, top
2. attractive; endearing.
   a winning smile
   - Similar: engaging, persuasive, charming, appealing, sweet, cute, pretty, attractive, lovely, captivating, enchanting, adorbs

/'winiNG/
Noun

1. money won, especially by gambling.

He went to collect his winnings.

- Similar: prize(s), money, gains, spoils, booty

Shplop!

My cold, wet bra falls on my face from the makeshift clothing line stretched across the narrow room, and my bunk jumps under me in an off-kilter way.

What in the unbuttered sourdough muffin is going on?!

Groggy and disorientated, my eyes open to darkness, the room tilting and water rushing in. I flail in the dark, panic surging through my veins as I roll, scrambling out of my bunk, and open the hatch into the dark hallway.

Chaos erupts as people rush past, shouting and shoving into the tiny space. My heart pounds, and my mind races as I fight against the crowd in the narrow hallway, trying to get up onto the ship's deck.

It's the Titanic! I'm in a death trap. I will drown stuck inside or die freezing in the arctic waters!

I must escape! My mind relives the movie scene with people falling off the rails into the gray, icy water—*OMG, why do I always default to the worst-case scenario?*

I see her, my Leonardo DiCaprio. She's a whirlwind of color and energy amidst the chaos-*Poppy*. My mind slows to take in the scene of Poppy wearing her comfy, brightly colored workout gear and hiking boots. Her caramel, sun-kissed skin, shiny black hair, and athletic physique make it impossible to mistake her for another crew member. Like me, she's an Alaskan indigenous woman. And she is also my secret summer crush.

"Come on, *Baby!*" Poppy calls out, her voice calm amid the panic. She grabs my hand and pulls me to the emergency exit.

I grasp her, my lifeline, as I stumble along to safety.

"It's Bailey," I whisper breathlessly and tighten my grip, securing my connection to her hand. Unlike Leo's character, dramatically releasing Kate, *I'm not letting go!*

Weeks ago, I got the courage to introduce myself to her, the most gorgeous crew member at the ship's Bon Voyage Mixer. I'm shy and barely talk to other crew members, and no one knew my name to introduce us, so I bravely approached her and introduced myself. But with the loud music, she misheard me and has called me "Baby" ever since.

I meant to correct her, but how she says *Baby* melts my heart, like drinking a hot dark mocha on a cold winter night. Since I never corrected her, and she's socially assertive, she *helpfully* introduced me to the rest of the crew. For weeks, I've been answering to the name *Baby.*

I'm changing my name. That's the obvious, least-embarrassing solution.

Poppy doesn't hear me. She kicks her hiking boot into a cabin door, whooping when it opens with a loud pop. Her vibrant brown eyes sparkle with determination, and her free-spirited laugh is out of place in this dire situation but entirely predictable for her. She propels people to the upper deck.

"Keep moving, Hector!" She shouts back to the dishwasher, whom I've never talked to before, let alone learned his name.

I bite my bottom lip-Correcting my name doesn't matter. Plus, I don't want to slow her-*us*-down, even though I'd like to go back and get my shoes and my phone. We reach the upper deck hatch together as icy water surges into the hallway, and I gasp as the cold water hits my bare legs.

Crack, a sharp noise hangs in the air as Poppy kicks another hatch open. Then, I am weightless for seconds when we plunge off the rails into the frigid waters of Kachemak Bay.

The shock of the cold water steals my breath. I cling to Poppy, who effortlessly treads water and keeps us afloat. Easy for her-she's a triathlete. I know because I'm stalking—I mean, *following*—her on social media, and sometimes I *accidentally* bump into her when she's working out on deck.

Together—*mostly her pulling us through the water*—we fight against the Arctic current, swimming toward the nearby rocky shoreline.

Thank God it's only two hundred meters away! As I tread the frigid water, a shiver races down my spine, back up my spine, and into my skull, causing my teeth to chatter incessantly. The icy ocean seeps through my pajamas and goosebumps my skin, numbing my feet and moving up my legs. My muscles tense in response to the biting cold, and tiny pins and needles dance through my body.

Is it possible to die of hypothermia while swimming to the nearby beach?

I'm still clinging to her with my death grip, and my toes probably have fallen off my feet since I no longer feel them.

I glance at the impressive Grewingk Glacier. We dropped our cruise guest off yesterday, and it's invisible in the dim morning. The tourists marveled at seeing the "real Alaska" and are tucked cozily at the Driftwood Lodge, where we were supposed to pick them up tonight in this bay overlooking Seldovia. The village of Seldovia is cast in a warm golden glow, nestled in the mountains and bordered by glaciers and the icy water I'm swimming in. The picturesque village's beauty starkly contrasts with the mess unfolding in the bay as the crew yells and the ship sinks.

My feet touch the rocks under the water, I gasp for breath, and I stumble with Poppy going the last five meters. *Perhaps I was overreacting a little, comparing this to the Titanic.*

As we reach the rocky shore, Poppy grins at me. "Baby, we made it, and the sun's coming up. Let's count this as our daily workout!" Then she laughs in pure relief, and I respond with a wordless smile.

I'm not dead! And Poppy holds me up as we crawl onto the rocky beach. If she releases me, my rubber legs will *for sure* give out. I also missed another opportunity to correct her.

It's actually Bailey—my enchanting mermaid—but you can call me Babycakes.

I'll tell her the first part when it's not an emergency. The second part, I'm keeping to myself!

As we stand here shivering and soaked, I'm in my sleepwear: a tank top and shorts. She's wearing her soaked heavy layers, a swimsuit, t-shirt, jeans, and hiking boots that didn't seem to slow her down during our swim.

Instead of being out of breath, she's exhilarated, and I can't deny the fluttering in my chest when she looks at me with her endless brown eyes and long raven hair fanned over her chest. Her vibrant spirit radiates warmth and strength despite our current situation.

She stops laughing to help pull up our other crew, crawling up the beach to join us.

"Look, it's the Titanic," a crew member points.

The colossal cruise ship, once a symbol of luxury and Arctic exploration, is listing at a dangerous angle. It defies logic, its form tilting as if the laws of physics are contorting under the weight of the calamity. I expect it to roll, but the ship dips and bobs before sinking into the bay like a killer whale, appearing and disappearing silently.

"That's... our belongings and our home!" My voice is calm, and the others' hysterical laughing evaporates. "How are we supposed to get paid?" Then I realize how selfish I sound and look at my feet, embarrassed. Of course, we lost our belongings, summer employment, and income, but we are alive and on the beach.

Poppy doesn't say anything about my comments. She meets my eyes, and her eyes mirror my disbelief. "Our summer jobs... They're gone, for sure. And there's no way we are getting our stuff.

"Reality punches me in the stomach, and I lean over dry heaving. *Thankfully, my stomach is pre-breakfast empty.* All my dreams of making enough money to fund my grad school tuition vanished just like our ship.

"We can't just stand here." Her voice refocuses me, and she helps me stand up from my failed vomiting. "We need to help. There are still people in the water. They could freeze before help comes."

As much as I admire her courage, swimming to the sinking ship is absurd. We are lucky not to be dead of hypothermia. "Poppy, no! You can't swim back out there. It's too dangerous."

Her eyes look at where the ship disappeared, and she looks through me and says, "I have to do something. I'm a strong swimmer. I can help."

"Are you out of your mind?" I say, my words cracking with panic. *If she swims out there, she's not returning.*

"You'll freeze out there, and what can you do even if you reach people? We need to find someone with a radio to call for help."

Another person, not a crew member, on the beach overhears and says, "There's no signal here. There's never a cell reception in Seldovia. We don't have any towers."

Panic churns in my stomach as the truth hits me—we're stranded, cut off from the world, unable to reach out for help, and stuck on this beach among strangers with only the wet, cold clothing on our backs.

Poppy puts her arm around me, and we look back to the water.

"Damn it!" I shake my head.

Poppy isn't alone in wondering what to do now. I notice the movement of locals coming onto the beach to see the activity in the bay.

A person wraps a heavy blanket around my shoulders, and before I can say thank you, the person moves on to hand a blanket to the next shivering crew member.

"Walk up there, and the volunteer firefighters can help you." A man points up the sloped beach, directing everyone to walk up the hill to town for help.

I don't want to swim out to our coworkers, but walking away feels like selfishly abandoning the crew stuck in the water and swimming to shore. We can only stand on the beach and shout for them to keep swimming.

Poppy grins, and her face lights up, pointing to the fishing boats chugging their way to rescue people. "See, Baby, the whole village is comin' to the rescue! Alaskans are always ready to lend a hand!"

I exhale and rub my hands together for warmth. My shoulders slump, and I bite my lip, kicking at a rock. "What are we supposed to do, then? Just stand here?"

"Don't worry. We'll figure it out!" Poppy puts her arm back over my shoulder, and we huddle on the beach watching.

What should we do about our situation?

Seldovia is an isolated little community that is not connected to the mainland except by boat. I can't drive, fly, or take a train home. I can't leave by a boat ferry with the bay and docks blocked. Worse, I have no money, phone, or family, and my parents don't expect to hear from me for weeks. They won't even realize I need help.

At least I don't need to reason with her not to dive back into the frigid water.

A sudden burst of commotion breaks through the gloom. A distant roar of engines grows steadily louder. A Coast Guard vessel emerges on the horizon, slicing through the bay.

I say, trembling slightly, "Thank goodness, the Coast Guard's here!"

A ripple of excitement courses through the crowd as the vessel draws closer. It's a majestic sight. Her hand finds mine, and we squeeze each other's fingers.

My hands are warm in hers and wrapped in the wool blanket.

The Coast Guard crew springs into action, deploying their rescue boats and reaching the shipwreck survivors still clinging to debris in the frigid water. Their efficiency and determination are astonishing.

We watch in awe as they pull our drenched crew members to safety. It's a moment of triumph and allows us to relax. Thank goodness Poppy won't be diving back into the ocean again.

She must have read my thoughts. "You know the water isn't that cold here. I take a thirty-minute swim in it on my training days."

"But you swim knowing a warm shower and coffee await you. Also, you're amazing," I say. "The rest of us aren't mermaids. We're more like sloths."

She shrugs her agreement, and we watch as the Coast Guard safely rescues the last crew member. A collective sigh washes over the beach, and we share smiles and high-fives. *We may have lost everything, but we've survived.*

Poppy and I smile, moving our fingers to lace together. The warmth of the blankets and coats chase away the beach's chilly winds. The wind doesn't seem too bad, and the cheering around us almost makes me forget that my toes are numb and we're stranded.

Oh. My. God. We are stranded here with no place to stay and no money!

A bystander's grim assessment reaches my ears, "Somebody must've messed up big time with those repairs. That ship went down fast."There's a grumbling agreement and relief that we didn't have any guests on board, and there doesn't appear to be any crew missing. The boat's emergency was unexpected, but we followed our training, and everyone made it out.

It's too bad the navigation crew and Captain are on the Coast Guard vessel-I'd like to give them a piece of my mind. *Who sinks a ship in calm waters near a dock?*

The weight of the situation bears down on me, suffocating my happiness at being so close to my crush and being alive.

Another voice jests, "Well, folks, this is Alaska's way of ending the tourist season. Go get coffee at the Visitor's Center or Fire Station. It's on the house!"

"Frank, the coffee is free there, and no one is going to charge them, anyways," a woman, who is probably Frank's wife, says, poking him.

A reluctant chuckle escapes my lips at the absurdity. The irony of the joke hits home—tourists are nowhere in sight, and our summer is over with our summer employment sinking along with the ship.

The other wet crew members wander up the hill into town with the helpful villagers. Poppy and I, still in a state of disbelief, stay behind and sit huddled together near the rocky shoreline, watching the sun rising and the bay filling with boats and strange equipment. The aftermath of the shipwreck leaves an air of uncertainty hanging over us, and sitting together in silence is comforting.

A figure stumbles towards us as if on cue, his uneven gait revealing his inebriated state. The smell of alcohol wafts from him, fouling the salt-laden breeze. He holds his breakfast beer loosely, the contents sloshing as he nears.

"Hey there, ladiesss," he slurs, his gaze shifting between us.

Poppy's arm tenses under my hand, her discomfort palpable. Linking my arm with hers, I send her a reassuring glance. We are together here."Hey," I reply cautiously. My voice's hesitancy matches the unsettling feeling in my gut.

The man's gaze lingers on Poppy, his eyes tracing her wet form in a way that makes my skin crawl. "You two are far from home, aren't ya?" he muses.

Her grip on my arm tightens, her instincts aligning with my own. "We're here for work," she replies.

He chuckles. "Work, huh? Well, the bay's gonna be closed until the Coast Guard's finnish, and I've got a boat. I'll take yous back to Homer, no skin off my nose, any."

His proposition and leering casts an ominous shadow over the already scary situation. The hairs on my neck prickle as I exchange a glance with Poppy.

Poppy stands. "No thanks.""We're okay," I add, my voice steady and my gut churning.

The man steps closer. "Come on now, sweethearts," he slurs. "You don't need to be alone. I can help yous out."

My grip on her arm tightens, and I dust the sand off my legs, leaving. With a forced smile, I nod toward the village. "We appreciate the offer, but we'll stick around here for a while. Enjoy your walk."

As we step away from his lingering gaze, the unease and the cold make me shiver. Poppy and I quickly walk opposite him, away from town and the almost empty beach. His threatening interaction ruins our excitement of being alive, and I'm tense and cold on a deserted beach.

My breath hitches, and my heart clenches, making me taste acid.

We're trapped in the wilderness—a place without rules, where danger lurks.

I link arms with Poppy, and she confidently walks, slowly navigating the unfamiliar wilderness with me since I'm barefoot with numb toes. As we walk away, the ocean drowns out the man's footsteps.

Chapter 2

Poppy's Winning Scheme

Strolling on the rugged shore, we're quiet, lost in our thoughts as the sun rises. Baby's anxious vibe is weighing her down—even I feel it. She's frowning at the rocky ground instead of savoring the pink and orange reflecting across the ocean. She chews on her lips, hiding her quirky smile.

I *must* lift her spirits. After all, optimism is my specialty, and choosing hope makes every situation bearable. *We are alive, on a beach with a beautiful sunrise—things could be much worse!*

"Poppy, what are we going to do?" Baby asks as we roam on the rugged shore, the morning stretching to afternoon.

I nudge her playfully. "Don't worry, Baby. Everything's gonna work out. Worrying won't change or help us. The sun is out, we have each other, and we'll figure it out."

My reassuring words are to lift her spirits and *mine*. We *are* in a sticky situation, stranded in this picturesque but unfamiliar part of Alaska. Without money or our phones, it's a little different than a usual hiccup when I travel.

The unknown and traveling to new places don't bother me because I'm training to be an elite triathlete. I travel all over to enter competitions, and I'm always in a strange place with no friends or family. Having the ship sink and being stranded is unexpected, and my competitive mind races to figure out how to win.

If only this were a test of strength or endurance, I know I'd be fine. I swim miles in the Arctic Ocean, trail run over mountains, and bike from Alaska to Canada, but our situation is vastly more complicated.

We need somewhere to sleep tonight and something to eat, then a way back home. *I won't even think about our lost jobs and our paychecks.*

"We could ask the locals for help," Baby suggests, her gaze flickering toward a small group of fishermen.

"The locals—like the guy offering us a ride?"

Baby bends down to pick a flat stone and skims it across the water. 1-2-3 skips. "Was it just me, or did he seem a little... creepy?"

I chuckle. "Oh yeah—definitely a *Creeper.* I doubt he even has a boat."

She looks out over the peaceful water. "But what about our summer work? Do you think we are even going to get paid for the summer cruise season now?"

I pick up the perfect flat round stone, toss it, and it skips eight times. Smiling, I pat her back. "We'll figure it out. Maybe we can find odd jobs around town or something. And hey, worst-case scenario, we could always work the *slime line* at the salmon cannery."

She wrinkles her nose at the thought of standing all day, cleaning the guts out of fish. The slime line is the lowest of the low of jobs in Alaska.

"I can't believe you'd even suggest that."

I wink and give her a grin. "Desperate times, my friend. But who knows, maybe we'll get lucky and stumble upon a pile of gold nuggets."

As if the gods heard my unasked prayer, there's a commotion ahead around the bend in the next little bay. A flurry of activity, cameras, and people scurrying around the beach grab our attention.

A surge of curiosity motivates me, and I gently grasp her arm, encouraging her to move closer. Destiny is providing, and I *refuse* to disregard an opportunity placed directly in our path.

"What in the world is happening over there?" Baby asks.

"Let's check it out," I say.

Amidst the buzz of activity, no one notices us wandering among the group despite our damp, odd appearance. We blend into the chaotic mix of people too engrossed in their own world to pay us any mind. Half of them are busy admiring their reflections on their phones, applying beauty products, while the others are preoccupied with their high-tech equipment. It's as if we are invisible in this sea of trendy, technology-obsessed individuals.

Dressed in jeans and shrouded in a weathered blanket, I wander into the fashionably dressed crowd. I wish I could stealthily acquire one of their shiny, brand-new puffer jackets and a sturdy pair of boots for Baby. She needs the extra warmth, and this touristy bunch wouldn't notice the absence of their photo props, the bright, name-brand cold-weather gear. Likely, they'll never wear it again after their obligatory vacation selfies for social media attention.

"I *must* get a selfie with a penguin," a blonde with two-inch manicured nails whines to another blondie, who responds by ignoring her and holding her phone up, trying to get unavailable cell reception.

Penguins are in Antarctica, not Alaska. This group's tour guide needs to educate these tourists seriously.

"When is the Director's ferry dropping him?" a young guy in the group, hunched over cameras, yells to another who is just as young but holding a clipboard, denoting his authority.

Mr. Clipboard, a Californian-cool guy with shades on despite the sun barely peeking through the clouds, scans the horizon and checks his watch. "He should be here any minute, guys. Let's shoot some nice opening shots and background shots. Go ahead and get started."

The guys exchange uncertain glances and shoulder shrugs as they set up to film the bay.

This group is clueless about the chaos just past their rocky beach; to be fair, they don't have a direct view of the bay around the corner. Even so, if one of them glanced further than the extent of their camera frames, they'd notice the boats rushing into the bay.

"Did you hear that guy?" Baby says, pointing to a huddle of men with expensive equipment filming the panoramic view of the ocean, mountains, and rocky beach.

"I was distracted by the women looking for penguins." I point to the group of stunningly beautiful women shivering, their sun-kissed blonde hair blown by the wind. They huddle together, forming a circle of golden-haired figures with rosy cheeks clad in stylish, albeit impractical, high-end fashion attire. Their designer parkas, heeled boots, and cashmere scarves do little to ward off the breeze.

Baby giggles with me. She says, "I overheard a snippet of conversation. They are filming and it's their first day."

Well, that explains the commotion and the odd assortment of people.

"It's got to be a reality show. But why out here on a remote beach?" I ask aloud.

She shrugs, and we notice a makeshift camp in the woods, complete with cameras, lights, and chairs lined up, like a movie set for some glamorous camping scene. The film crew left a big rack of tourist winter gear: overly warm skiing puffer jackets, fleece layers, useless Ugg boots, and hats announcing brand names.

It looks like the wardrobe crew left some goodies for us. I'm sure they wouldn't miss a few items.

Who are these filming tourists? I glance at the white-skinned, blonde-haired bunch, shivering in the warm weather.

An Alaskan visit from the Housewives of California? American Idol tryouts in a unique location?

"Should we ask them what they're doing? They look like they need Alaskan guides," she adds thoughtfully.

"We definitely know the area better than them. I spy the breakfast spread. Let's check that out first." I hook Baby's arm, and we meander from the two groups to tables and RVs in the woods behind the beach.

I can't shake the feeling this is an opportunity as we venture closer. Our stomachs rumble, and we enjoy the abandoned table spread with muffins, fruit, and coffee. *I doubt most of these blondies even eat carbs.*

I snag a muffin and pass one to Baby. "Well, look at us, scavengers in the wild. At least we won't starve."

She takes a bite of the blueberry muffin. "Desperate times call for desperate measures," she says, more determined than anxious.

Baby's cute when she gets motivated! I nudge her and give her a wink.

As we nibble on our impromptu meal and sneak on some fleece ski vests, I unfold a paper, reading:

!!!FOR THE DIRECTOR'S EYES ONLY!!!

The Smoking Hot, Arctic Bachelor

**Description:*

Get ready for the ultimate Alaskan adventure as ten fearless, beautiful bachelorettes battle it out to win the heart of our very own Arctic bachelor, BURLY! Join us as we take you on a wild ride through the untamed wilderness, where love, passion, and survival skills are put to the test. With Alaskan challenges and steamy, passionate romance, this is one ruggedly unique dating show.

<u>Bachelorette Challenges:</u>

1. "Iceberg Surfing": Contestants must ride icebergs in frigid waters while attempting to stay balanced. The last one standing wins. Bikinis or formal dresses are preferred for Bachelorettes.

2. "Polar Plunge Date": Bachelorettes go on a date in sub-zero temperatures, dressed in skimpy bathing suits, and must take a dip in an ice-cold Arctic ocean to win time with the Bachelor.
3. "Snow Sculpting Showdown": Contestants create intricate snow sculptures using only their hands and essential tools. The most creative sculpture wins.
4. "Salmon Wrestling": Bachelorettes will fish, catching and wrestling live salmon with their bare hands in a freezing river alongside grizzly bears fishing.
5. "Blizzard Blindfold Challenge": Contestants are blindfolded and dropped during a snowstorm. They must find their way back to camp without any assistance.
6. "Extreme Northern Lights Dance": Bachelorettes compete in a dance-off under the Northern Lights, where they incorporate their best Arctic dance moves into their sexy routines.
7. "Eskimo Fashion Show": Contestants have to create stylish outfits from materials found in the Arctic, such as wild seal fur and icicles, and then strut their stuff on an icy runway.

8. "Avalanche Escape": Bachelorettes are placed in a simulated avalanche scenario and must work together to escape before the "snow" engulfs them.
9. "Arctic Cooking Challenge": Contestants must cook a gourmet meal using only ingredients they can scavenge from the wilderness: aprons and chef hats per Costume Designer.

These challenges will test the Bachelorettes' beauty, commitment, and adaptability while providing plenty of entertaining, authentic Alaskan moments for the viewers.
Adapt challenges to the environment and materials available—winner (s) to be chosen by the Director or Arctic Bachelor, Burly.
Timeline:
Two weeks of heart-pounding Arctic challenges, romantic rendezvous, and unexpected twists. Who will withstand the elements and capture the heart of our Northern Arctic Bachelor?
Winner Payout:
Our lucky lady will win the chance at true

love with our Arctic Wilderness Bachelor and walk away with the generous cash prize of $50,000!

(Winner TBA by the Director)

!!!EMPHASIZE: THE INTENSE DRAMA, SULTRY ROMANCE, AND UNEXPECTED VICTOR!!!

"Are they *for real?*" She asks, looking over my shoulder. "This is ridiculous!"

I shake my head, trying to talk over my bubbling laugh. "Did you read the *challenges* list? It's like they think Alaska is a big winter wonderland, all year!"

She rolls her eyes and laughs. "Seriously, *iceberg surfing* and *snow sculpting* in the middle of summer? They clearly did no research before coming here."

I can't stop laughing, and she quiets me by pulling the blanket over our heads before we draw attention.

"And don't even get me started on the *Polar Plunge Date.* We just swam in the bay, it's not something I see any of those women doing for fun!" she adds.

I look at the woefully unprepared contestants. Seriously, I can't imagine any of those stylish models fishing, hiking, and *definitely not iceberg surfing!* I would watch a show that teaches them to ice fish and build a makeshift shelter. It would be hilarious!

"Yep, those poor ladies have no clue what they've gotten into. It's too bad because I could win this against them."

She raises an eyebrow. "You're not seriously considering entering and winning an Arctic reality show, are you?"

I pause. *I wasn't—until she mentioned it.* "Oh, I am. And *we* are entering! We'll use our Alaskan knowledge and teamwork to outshine these other bachelorettes. Plus, it's $50,000! That's a fortune, more than winning first place at an international triathlon. You need this money for grad school and I need it to start my triathlete career. We'll split it."

"You're crazy, Poppy."

I look at her and lift my eyebrow, giving her my most conspiring look with a grin.

She laughs and then looks at the huddle of princesses. Shrugging, she says, "I guess, I can't end summer without my grad school money– I'm in!"

I smile and clap. "Yes! Let's show them what *real* Alaskan women are made of."

We have a plan. Winning this gameshow is *way more* money than we would've made working on the cruise ship.

She smiles, scrunching her nose.

I grab the papers off the table, scribble her name under "contestant," and hand it to her. "That's the spirit! Now, let's fill out these applications and join our competitors."

Before we iron out our plan, the clipboard manager waves at us. "You two, over here!"

We look at each other and nod, walking over to him. He's tired, and a name tag identifies him as Conner, the "Producer."

Conner's eyes flick between us, his gaze lingering on Baby for a moment longer. "You ladies are here for the show, right?"

"Of course!" I say, giving him my dazzling smile.

He smiles back. "Great! I knew you two were our local contestants. Finish your forms so we can head to camp. We are starting without the Director and Host, but at least we have all ten contestants."

I whisper to Baby, "It's time for *full Alaskan mode*, okay?"

Entertaining tourists on the cruise sometimes means stretching the truth about being Alaskan, like how we live in igloos and travel by dog sled. The crew jokes that this is *full Alaskan mode*. Tourists love it, and we get great tips when we tell them about our fictitious wild Alaskan lives.

She nods and flips through the application, which looks more like a dating application than a work form.

I scribble, filling in the blanks with my weight and hobbies. I wink at Baby. "Guess who's an iceberg yoga instructor among the whales on Glacier Bay?"

With a giggle and her quirky smile back, she responds, "Really? I took you for an Arctic canoe guide who dreams of settling down on an Alaskan homestead making rose hip jam for your twenty children."

Our laughter catches the attention of Conner. "Glad to hear laughing. The other contestants are complaining about the cold weather."

He's distracted by an Alaskan beaver fur hat on a crew member. "Can we get that hat in faux fur? Fur is so 2000– no fur on the set!"

As we hurriedly finish filling out the sheets, I glance at the women gathering in camp. They're striking, each one more attractive than the last. The realization hits me - we're about to compete against some seriously stunning women.

I look at my filthy clothes. *I hope this Alaskan guy is looking for more than a blonde with boobs.*

Baby's motivated and snatches my sheet, handing it to Conner so we can join the others in front of the yurts.

Walking away, I overhear Conner talking to a crew member. "Every dating reality show needs an ugly girl and an underdog- you know, for the viewers to root for."

Baby hears, too. She frowns and turns to me. "Am I the ugly one or the underdog?"

"Neither! It doesn't matter what he thinks, remember. We'll charm the Alaskan guy, Burly, and the Director to win."

She nods and smiles, her lips free from biting them with worry.

I'm happy her anxiety is gone, and she's back to her bubbly self. She's shy, but underneath, I see the effervescent, intelligent person she is.

I look around at the shivering, unhappy, beauty-pageant women.

"Baby, you're going to be the winner!"

Chapter 3

Baby's Unspoken Desires

"Okay, Bachelorettes, gather around!" Conner's voice booms, cutting through the crisp Alaskan air. His sunglasses are on his head, and his gleaming, supernatural white teeth make me squint.

Poppy is smiling, confidently ready. But I can't help but wonder if we've bitten off more than we can chew. *Can we really pull this off?*

"Shouldn't we wait for the Director?" one of the younger crew members asks.

"We've got a show to make. And I will Direct until my father-er, the *Director*, shows up. We are burning light and money. Keep the film rolling, and the edit team will deal with it," he responds with a toss of his blond hair and a Californian surfer attitude.

"The first challenge," he continues, turning to us, "is all about *roughing it* in the great outdoors and making the *rough* Arctic yurt your safe wilderness home-away-from-home."

He surveys the group and continues. "You'll need to pick a partner and a yurt. Once you've done that, it's time to bear-proof it. The team that wins at making their yurt the most bear-safe wins a private first impression date with our ruggedly handsome Arctic Bachelor before everyone else. Remember what you're competing for, the highly-coveted First Impression Date, which might just win you the heart of our most eligible bachelor in Alaska. Good luck!"

There's a collective groan from the other contestants, but Poppy's eyes are alight with determination. She's fiercely competitive, and I'm grateful for her confidence right now.

"I don't want a *rough tent-thing.* I want a hotel suite!" a bachelorette wearing a tiara and pink earmuffs grumbles.

As we start making our way toward the yurts, the complaints and protests from the other girls increase.

"This is ridiculous!" another says, "Bear-proofing? I thought we were supposed to be the cougars, not be hunted by bears! This is a dating show, right? I want a king-sized canopy bed filled with furs." The other contestants nod and agree with her.

Poppy squeezes my hand, her gaze on the yurts ahead. "We've got this, Baby. We're Alaskans! According to them, we live in the wilderness among dangerous predators already."

I nod, but doubt flickers in my mind. *What if they find us out, and Conner kicks us off the show? Is the Coast Guard still around to take us home?*

We reach the yurts and join the scramble as the other girls pick their partners and claim their *wilderness home-away-from-home.* The choosing criteria are identical to school gym class: popularity and looks. No one approaches us to partner.

Poppy and I pick an empty yurt on the edge of camp. The view is incredible, with the ocean in front of us and the forested mountains behind us. The pristine wilderness and pine scent surround us. Conner may not know anything about Alaska, but the show's Location Scout picked a beautiful backdrop for the show.

"This place is incredible," I whisper to Poppy.

She nods, her eyes scanning the yurt for potential weaknesses. "It is. But we can't let it distract us from the challenge."

As we start bear-proofing our yurt, the film crew is nearby, their cameras pointing at a bear crossing sign.

Are they seriously waiting for a bear to cross at the sign?

"Hey, Poppy, look over there." I nudge her and point to the crew filming Conner sitting on a log, leaning to the camera, explaining the dangers of rabid, hungry predators living in the Arctic. He stops talking and glances behind his shoulder, where the sign is out of the shot but next to him.

"They *are!* They are seriously waiting to film a bear." I shake my head.

"No! They can't think bears read signs and cross right where the signs are located."

The crew members scratch their heads and look at their watches and the nearby woods, still filming beside the large, yellow bear crossing sign.

I smack my forehead and sigh.

"We are *so* going to win this! I hope they brought bear spray," Poppy says with a wide smile.

We work to bear-proof our yurt, which is easy since we have nothing to attract bears, so they won't bother it. But as I glance around, I see the crew filming the others, skipping us. I realize the other teams are taking a different approach. The other girls are tying bells around their yurts, creating makeshift spears, and placing rocks around their doors as if they could prevent a bear from entering with a spear or stones.

"Poppy," I say, "I think we're doing this all wrong. Look at them—tying bells around their yurts and making weapons. We are being too Alaskan. We should compete like Hollywood expects Alaskans to be- full Alaskan style."

She stops hanging a rope from a nearby tree, creating a safe food storage place away from our yurt. She meets my eyes, a spark of understanding, and she nods. "You're right, Baby. I was thinking about bear-proofing and not about who is judging us."

Before we can change strategies, Conner announces the time is up, and we stand by our yurt.

"No early warning system, no defenses planned, and you choose the yurt farthest away from camp and closest to the dangerous, unforgiving wilderness filled with deadly predators." He shakes his head and moves on to the next yurt.

This challenge *was not* about our Alaskan knowledge. The challenge *was* about impressing Conner and the film crew. The team wearing the skimpiest outfits is getting the most points.

As the film crew sets up to announce the winner, Poppy says, "Come with me." She removes her shirt, revealing her athletic chest and arms hugged by her black swimsuit.

I'm breathless.

"Hey, I have something for you to film." She bats her eyelashes at the crew, and I have no clue what she's up to.

They center the camera on her, and she pulls her hair down around her shoulders, looking absolutely smoldering. She looks at me. "Hey Baby."

I raise my eyebrows. "Yeah."

"You know how you recognize bear poop in Alaska, right?"

I smile because this is a joke we tell the cruise boat tourists. "How?"

"Well, there's bells in it," she erupts, and the crew and her laugh raucously together.

She may have won over the film crew with her flirty banter, but Conner doesn't look.

He pauses to announce the winner. "Emily and Quartz win a first impression meeting with our hunky Arctic Bachelor tonight!" he says.

Ugh! They were the team with the most bells and skimpiest outfits. The Director's sheet did say to emphasize *sultry.*

Poopy narrows her eyes and loops her arm in mine. "No worries. We know how to compete now. We've got the playbook and the advantage. We'll win the next one."

I bite my lip and smile at her raised chin, exposing her long neck and strong shoulders. My cheeks flush, and I turn away to hide the heat.

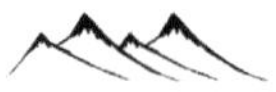

The last of the sunlight streams through the circular opening at the top of the yurt, casting a warm glow over our temporary home. It's cozy and modest. Two single beds, a small table, and a flickering lantern, provide comfort in the rustic set-up. There's no electricity or water, and outhouses by the woods for bathrooms. Despite *roughing it,* the yurt's inside is bigger than the size of our rooms on the cruise, and the bedding is warm, even with the chill outside the fabric walls. Additionally, the crew keeps a fire lit with plenty of hot drinks and snacks in the middle of camp.

Our camp set-up is nothing like *roughing it:* sleeping in a tent on the ground, unable to light the mossy, damp wood for a fire, and trying to fish for my dinner, akin to roughing it camping with my family when I was younger. This is plush and a lovely, oceanside *wilderness home-away-from-home,* as Conner says.

I sit on the edge of my bed, my hands gripping the rough woolen blanket, watching as Poppy paces the limited space, her athletic figure outlined by the soft lantern light. She talks out our strategy to win.

"We are at a disadvantage because we only have what we're wearing, and we can't exactly explain that we snuck onto their show. Also, there's the whole romance thing—I'm not here to fall in love, but we need to get him to fall in love with one of us." She stops pacing and looks at me for agreement.

I nod, though a pang of disappointment settles in my chest. I secretly hope sharing this yurt will bring us closer, and she'll develop feelings for me. But obviously, she's focused on winning.

"I get it," I reply. "I'm in the same boat. Grad school doesn't pay for itself, and I need the money."

Her dark eyes meet mine. "So, we must stay focused and do whatever it takes to win."

I admire her resolve, even as I wish for more. "Absolutely," I agree.

A sudden thought crosses my mind, and it is now or never to share my secret. "Poppy, there's something you should know about me."

She turns. "What is it, Baby?"

I take a deep breath, my heart pounding, and I cross my fingers, hoping this isn't going to change our deal. "So, I'm a lesbian."

The confession hangs in the air, and she licks her lips, then begins pacing again. "Okay," she says calmly. "Thanks for sharing."

Relief washes over me. Her reaction is *much* better than I feared.

She adds, "I'm not exactly into Alaskan men either. I think of my sexuality as fluid. I'm *situationally sexual.* I don't do labels or genders. I just take each situation as it comes."

I nod and smile. *I have a chance!*

"Our strategy doesn't change. We still need to attract the bachelor and win. Let's focus on the next challenge and do not tell anyone about your sexuality," she says, pacing again and strategizing.

"But if the situation arises for you. . ." I trail off, hoping she'll be open to romance with someone besides the Arctic Bachelor.

She pauses pacing and faces me with her set jaw, steepled fingers, and a wide stance. "My focus is solely on this competition. All our focus and energy need to be on winning. When competing, I have no energy for passion or feelings. That's the deal," she responds.

Her answer crushes my hopes. I nod and hide my disappointment with a smile. "I understand."

"Baby, I appreciate your honesty. We need to be a team, which means we should fake being *hetero-vanilla* and lusting after an Arctic man for the sake of this competition. Can you do that for me?"

The question is more of a statement, and I nod back. I know what's at stake. This ridiculous situation is our chance to win money for our dreams. As strong as they are, my feelings for Poppy could get in the way of us winning.

"No problem," I say. "I love hairy, outdoorsy Alaskan men, and sign me up for that iceberg race!"

She smiles. "That's the attitude. You're an amazing friend, and we will make a winning team."

I half smile back at my *friend*, her label of me. *But this competition doesn't have to be terrible.* I get to hang out with Poppy in this fantastic camp, and my dreams are within reach.

Even if I can't find love, I'll help Poppy win. And winning this competition lets me finish grad school, and that's what I really want.

Poppy tosses her long black hair over her shoulder, and I clench in a spot lower than my knotted stomach.

She's so gorgeous! There's no way Burly won't fall in love with her at first sight. I just want a chance to win over my *situational sexual* friend's heart during the next two weeks.

But... we have a competition to win, and Poppy wants my focus to be unwavering. She deserves to achieve her dreams, and I will do everything I can to ensure she does.

Chapter 4

Poppy, the Kleptomaniac

The blinding light hits me squarely in the eyes. "Rolling!"

Seriously, do they need to shine a spotlight directly into my retinas? I blink and try not to make a face.

Conner says, "It's all about *YOU,* Poppy! Don't worry about the sheet. Tell us everything about you—but make it sexier, more dramatic." He looks down at my application.

Oh God!

Before my morning coffee, I can't recall the wild Alaskan stories I wrote there. *Did I write that I tagged and tracked Narwhals?*

"She should do some yoga poses to establish shots and set the scene," I hear a guy whisper to Conner.

Ah, yes—I'm an iceberg-riding yoga instructor. I better distract them with my Alaskan introduction because I may injure myself trying yoga for the first time. I'm athletic, but that's different than flexibility.

Luckily, he's interrupted by a crew member bringing him a satellite phone.

I take a breath, and a make-up and hair person rushes over to apply powder, lip gloss, and then some smelly potion to my hair. I'd refuse, but having someone fuss over me is a different and pleasant experience. I'm not a girly girl or modelesque like the Bachelorettes around me, but I'm tall and lean, and my luscious black hair gets compliments wherever I go.

She fluffs it and twists it into loose waves as I catch snippets of Conner's call.

"...Dad... I'll just let Burly pick the winner....No, it's fine...they'll get their ten episodes...Yes, Dad. I got this," Conner says, his voice laced with determination.

I look around, and no one else is nearby to hear Conner except me and the powdering crew member. If everyone else thinks Conner or the no-show Director is picking the winner, I'll have an advantage knowing they leave it solely up to Burly. I smile with my shiny lips and lift my chin.

"Honey, you are gorgeous. If you don't have a contract already, I know an agency that'd put you on covers tomorrow," the woman says, adding another layer of gloss to my lip. "Those lips and your natural beauty. Girl, you're the real deal!"

I blush, and she steps back, cocking her head to survey her work. *She must compliment all the contestants.* But I sit taller and smile.

He steps back behind the camera. "Poppy, go ahead and give us a Mountain Pose with a Twist while you do your introduction," Conner directs, "And just your leotard, please."

I cringe inside and give my best *full-Alaskan* smile with a flutter of my lashes.

Twister Mountain pose? Leotard?

I glance down, realizing Conner's request pertains to the black swimsuit concealed beneath my shirt and jeans, pulling double duty as a makeshift bra and a substitute tank top. My bust is rather assertive, eagerly signaling *Good Morning* this crisp morning.

Why not? I shrug out of my fleece jacket and jeans, putting my hair over my shoulder.

Naturally, Conner's well-versed in yoga poses. This whole crew and the ladies seem to hail from sunny California*! I wouldn't be surprised if he's into Pilates and that peculiar pole-dancing trend repackaged as an athletic workout.*

I look directly at the camera, unblinking. I push out my chest, standing tall and trying to remember the poses the tourists do on the ship's deck for pictures. I lunge, spread my arms, and then reach my arm toward the mountains in the distance. I flash my most winning smile at the camera. "I'm Poppy, and I'm thrilled to be able to teach people the ancient and beautiful art of yoga. I teach among the narwhales of the Arctic." I breathe out and bring my arm slowly down with a smile.

"Warrior two is fine. Now blur her and capture the mountain behind."

I freeze with a smile, and the film crew fiddles with knobs.

"That's perfect!" Conner says, looking at the screen on the camera.

I sigh - *they believed I was a morning-leotard-wearing Alaskan yoga instructor.*

"Keep talking and pretend you are talking directly to your one true love, the Arctic Bachelor."

"Um. . ." I stall, not recalling what other crazy facts I wrote down. Being the first awake, the crew snagged me and put me in front of the cameras before I got my coffee. I'm a morning person, but my brain needs a daily caffeine shot.

I see other Bachelorettes waking up, and I missed the dress code memo because it is a glamping, sexy, urban chic vibe. My old t-shirt and jeans will stick out like a sore thumb among the tight yoga pants, halter tops, ankle boots, and sandals.

Quartz mumbles, "No one said to bring our Barreto Dancewear for silhouette shots."

"Not that our silhouette would look that amazing, though," Emily responds and winks at me as they gawk.

He interrupts, waving dismissively. "No worries, Poppy. Just say what I tell you."

Right. I clear my throat, feeling like the starting gun just went off, and I'm not on the diving platform. I'm unprepared for this, but I'll pull myself together. We are in a competition, and I *win* competitions!

"Okay, action!" The acting director snaps his fingers, and I smile as the camera zooms into my face. He writes lines on an oversized sheet of paper and holds it behind the camera, pointing to his mouth and then miming a huge smile.

"Hi, I'm Poppy, like the flower," I begin. "I'm ready to make sparks fly, even in sub-zero temperatures. Between canoeing and collecting wildflowers, I've been searching for a piece of my missing heart. Being chosen for Arctic Bachelor is a dream, and I can't wait to meet Burly! Alaska's cold, but my red-hot love is real and ready to melt his heart."

I mentally cringed at their description of me. My crazy-fake *full Alaskan mode* description I wrote doesn't come close to this level of saccharine fake.

I want to win, though. I shoot a pouty half-smile to the camera and bat my eyelashes.

Baby comes over with an extra coffee and watches, her shoulders shaking to hold the laughter inside.

Thank god! Coffee!

“Poppy, you missed a line. Read this very slowly and show us authenticity—some *real* passion.“ He holds up the paper again.

“I am more stunning than the Northern Lights above,” I say slowly and breathlessly, looking at the camera with a pout, pretending to be a sultry yoga instructor. “Trust me, I’ll warm you up on the coldest night.”

If Burly and the game show want a lovesick, cheesy woman, then that’s what I am.

I’m going to win, whatever it takes!

My cheeks burn, and I run my hand through my hair, waiting for the film crew to stop and pick another victim-*contestant*-to film.

“Cut! Great,” he says and dismisses me with a wave.

I get up, pull on my clothes, and join Baby for a coffee.

She says, “You *are* more stunning than the Northern Lights.”

“Get some shots of the Northern Lights for the background,” I hear a crew member say.

I glance around, confused.

Northern Lights? It’s daytime in the summer—there are no Northern Lights to film.

We giggle as the crew check their watches and grumble. “Where are those Northern Lights? Are they late?”

“Should we tell them?” Baby asks.

"No way. I just escaped," I say, "Let's get some more coffee and see how the other girls do."

"We need to plan my sappy intro," she adds.

"How about: *They say snowflakes are all beautiful and unique, and that's how my love is?*" I raise my brows at her.

She laughs. "Or, *I love to hike, and I will find the map to the Bachelor's heart and hike the snowy peaks for him.*"

"Ohhhh, that one's good. You are a natural!"

Baby is good at joking and flirting when she's not hiding, trying to blend into the wallpaper during gatherings.

She won't need Conner to feed her lines.

"But say it with smoldering eyes and bite your cute lower lip," I say, winking.

She giggles with me as we enjoy sitting on a log by the fire. We watch the chaos as the other contestants try to apply makeup without mirrors and tools in the woods. I never knew it was so difficult to look natural. Apparently, wilderness camping makeup involves earth tones, adding freckles, and clear lip gloss, per their conversations.

"Chloe! Kimmy! Who's next?" Conner yells as the two blondes poking their heads out hide back inside their yurt.

"Hey, get some clips of the Alaskan girls bonding by the fire," Conner calls, motioning the crew to us.

"Uh oh. We've been spotted," Baby says.

"That's okay." I put my arm around her, and we smile for the camera as they shoot us drinking coffee and poking a stick at the fire.

"Maybe you should pour maple syrup in your coffee," a crew member suggests.

"That's a Canadian thing, man." Another crew member laughs.

I call out, "I'm game. Bring on the syrup, eh!"

We continue to giggle in front of the fire as the other bachelorettes prepare to film their introductions. The production crew is busy wrangling and calming them down when they realize we only have an outhouse and no indoor plumbing in the woods.

"I don't think we need to do much to win. Look at them already," I say, pointing. The other girls are tripping over roots in their heels, swatting at the mosquitos, and grumbling about not having electricity for their beauty routine.

Conner must have read my thoughts because his amused gaze meets mine as he tries to direct the crew to film back to filming the Bachelorettes prepping. And the blonde waking Bachelorettes are hiding, refusing to allow filming without looking perfect. He shakes his head.

I shrug and exchange a smile with him as we enjoy watching the morning circus of the other bachelorette's utter confusion about getting ready at camp.

Suddenly, a chorus of screams erupts as a cloud of wasps descends upon a group huddled around the coffeemaker, where they plugged in someone's flat iron and a lit mirror.

"Film that!" Conner shouts rather than helping the screaming contestants.

"Their perfumes attracted them," I say, standing up to help as Emily tries to run by.

I hook her arm. "Come by the fire. The smoke keeps them away."

She looks at me with teary eyes and smeared lipstick, nodding and sitting close to the flames. And I debate if she's safer away from the wasp or near the fire, as her hairspray and shiny pants make her highly flammable.

"Just leave them alone, and they won't sting," Baby calls out as the other contestants frantically swat at the bugs. The word *sting* incites more screaming, though.

I shake my head in disbelief. These city girls have no idea what they're getting into. Meanwhile, Baby and I watch the commotion, sipping our coffee and wondering where the medic is. There's a medical station by the kitchen tent. A medic would tell them to stop hitting the wasps and calm down!

"Those skimpy outfits and heels," Baby says, shaking her head.

"The intro is a crucial part of this, you know," Emily says, explaining, "The social influencers and the models want to be seen and sponsored, so of course, they are wearing dresses and heels."

"Sorry. It's just a bad idea," Baby says as we watch. "I know they're our competition, but can someone tell them not to wear perfume?"

"They'll figure it out," Emily says, grabbing our arms to keep us away from helping them and by the fire.

Everyone here is out for themselves, except Baby and I!

"Baby and I want to hear about Burly. What was he like?" I ask Emily since she won the First Impression Date along with Quartz.

Her eyes light up, and she clutches her heart. "He's ooh-so ruggedly handsome and charming. It's like he's the Alaskan James Bond or something. I only got a minute with him, but it was totes magical, and boom-instalove."

She smiles and hugs herself as Baby rolls her eyes at me. With the screaming calming down, Emily gets up to finish getting ready and leaves me and Baby alone again.

"I hope he's as down-to-earth as he is good-looking. We might have some tough competition if he likes blondes with floral scent," Baby says.

"We are different and stand out, so that'll help us," I add.

"Once he meets a girl who's *more stunning than the Northern Lights,* none of us stand a chance with him," she jokes, and we erupt in giggles.

"You forgot about how I'm *sooooo hot. I'll heat up his heart and his bed!"*

Conner's voice breaks through the commotion as the camera crew finishes capturing the chaos. "Alright, ladies, let's regroup and get back to filming intros. But I appreciate the fake distress- remember, authenticity is the name of the game!"

They aren't pretending, though.

The contestants have holed up in their yurts, seeking refuge.

The pink, tiara-wearing contestant storms over to Conner, her expression lethal.

"I'm done!" she yells, her voice carrying over the camp. "The bugs, the dirt, these huts, and no electricity—*It's abuse!* I didn't sign up for *this*!"

Her outburst draws the other Bachelorettes out to watch, and the filming crew members exchange glances, then they refocus their lenses and point their cameras at her. Among the Bachelorettes, she stands out, a *Pink Princess,* from her extravagant, brightly pink-themed wardrobe. Despite the directions to dress "natural," she's in a shocking fuchsia gown and tiara.

Conner approaches her calmly. "We understand that it's challenging," he says, trying to defuse the situation. "But this is part of the experience. We're all in this together. And you have a chance at love, fame, and money in this beautiful Arctic game show."

"Screw this!" She storms off, shouting, "I'm not sleeping here. I'm checking into a hotel with a hot shower!"

The other contestants watch in nail-biting silence, torn between sympathy and contemplating joining her.

As *Princess* parades away from camp, tripping as her heels dig into the dirt, her figure disappears over the hillside to Seldovia. No one else joins her or rushes to stop her, either.

Baby says, "Shashay Away," and Conner looks over with a sly grin and chuckles with her.

Princess' announcement sends shockwaves through the camp. Contestants whisper among themselves, and the crew scrambles to adjust to the unexpected turn of events. Her abrupt departure threatens to disrupt the carefully crafted narrative of the light-hearted game shows. But this show thrives on drama, so they have a dramatic first episode before we even meet our Bachelor, Burly.

We've only been *roughing it* camping in the woods one night and already losing contestants. I hope the other bachelorettes are more prepared than her. *Or maybe not-since this makes winning easier.*

I squeeze Baby's hand with encouragement. We are one contestant closer to winning, and I am more focused than ever. We exchange glances.

"One down, seven prom queens left," I whisper.

Conner asks the filming crew, "Did you catch all that?"

They nod and lean over the camera viewer to rewatch the scene unfold.

"Great. I love the backdrop and end with that shot," he says, unphased by the unexpected early departure. "It's perfect. Two contestants, holding their hands in unity against the dangerous wilderness and their friend's departure."

I look down, and my hand is holding Baby's in front of the fire.

"Good news, not only am I *more stunning than the Northern Lights,* but I'm also a *kleptomaniac.* Look what I got us." With a grin, I unveil the pink left-behind suitcase I swiped from Princess's yurt.

"Please let there be some underwear, sweats, and socks in there," Baby prays, her eyes open and hopeful.

"You do know that this is Princess I-Don't-Do-Camping's bag. I'll be happy if there's a dress and bra that fit,"

I jest. "Do you want to do the honors?" I point at the pink zippers.

She claps her hands. "It's a Christmas surprise—in August!" She moves the oversized bag onto her bed and gently unzips it.

"Tada," she declares, revealing an array of pink-colored items packed for a Paris runway show, *not* for camping in Alaska.

I move the pink mirror and curling iron to uncover the rainbow of pink-colored thongs, a bronzer kit, glue-on fake lashes—*Seriously, who brings these things to the wilderness?*—and a bottle of Pure Honey Kim Kardashian.

I picked up the bottle. "Was her main goal to attract the bugs and bears?"

Our laughter mingles with the rustling of fabrics as we unearth a pink toothbrush travel kit, pink packaged face wipes, and the last item, a pink manicure kit with a sparkling silver polish labeled "Polar Kissez."

"Well, we have underwear now," I remark, flinging a thong playfully at her, and we both burst into a fit of laughter as we slingshot the thongs at each other.

"You know," I muse, snagging the sparkly nail polish, "I really do want to win this, not just for the money but for a chance to prove myself. Emily's right. If major sporting companies see me swimming and hiking on the show, they might sponsor me for upcoming triathlons. This whole disastrous summer would be worth it."

Baby bites her plump bottom lip, and she nods. "That's true. Some people die to be on TV, and you never know where this could lead. Maybe Burly will be super-hot and a triathlete. You could be a perfect match and not even have to fake it."

"Or he could tempt you from your *sinful lesbian ways* and make you Mrs. Burly," I tease her, slingshotting a nearby lace thong at her head, and she blushes, ducking.

I open the polish, and we relax, painting each other's nails.

I wiggle my sparkly toes as Baby blows on them. *Maybe this is our good luck charm.*

Being on a reality dating show wasn't in my top million things to do, but it's kinda fun to sneak onto the show with a friend. Her warm breath tickles my feet, and I try not to squirm.

Although, aside from winning the cash prize, there's *no chance* I'd fall in love.

I wiggle my lucky, tickly toes at Baby, with her red lips pressed together in concentration as she moves to paint my fingers.

I can still have fun, though!

Chapter 5

Baby's Fear

The small lantern's fire casts shadows in our cozy yurt, and I blow on Poppy's toenails, expediting the drying process. "I can't believe we're painting our nails in the middle of the wilderness."

She shivers and grabs a wool blanket. "Hurry! It's getting cold tonight."

She's right, I think, as the wind gusts against our yurt. The girl time bonding with the stolen polish is fun, but it's getting too cold to enjoy it. I grab my blanket and cocoon myself while we wait for our nails to dry.

"*Funny story*-Emily asked if I could have my *friends* drop off a cellphone signal booster. She snuck in a phone but doesn't have a signal. She begged for her *two hundred thousand plus followers,* who are *her close family,*" Poppy says, shaking her head.

"*Nooo!* First off, that's a crazy amount of supposed f*amily*—what does her Christmas family photo look like?" Counting off my four fingers, I say, "Second, we have no cell towers or electricity. Thirdly, she flew into Anchorage, drove the six hours, and took a boat here.

Does she think there's a shortcut or city nearby that everyone chooses to ignore because we enjoy the one to two-day trip here?"

"Wait. She did nicely offer that I could use the phone too," she says, "What's the fourth thing?" She tilts her chin at my remaining finger.

"The fourth thing is, I can't count, and it's getting super windy out there." I laugh as a gust of wind shakes our yurt.

Poppy laughs and puts a thong over her head like earmuffs. "You want a pair of my designer ear warmers?" She giggles and winks at me.

I bite my bottom lip and ask, "Maybe we should push our bunks together?" I hold my breath, hoping she'll agree. Our focus is on winning, but we can cuddle, *just a little—as friends, right?*

She gives me a mischievous grin. "Are you suggesting we cuddle to stay warm, Baby?"

A warmth rises to my cheeks, and I shrug with nonchalance. "Hey, desperate times call for desperate measures, right?"

Poppy laughs and scrunches her nose.

I haven't summoned the courage to confess my real feelings to her. It doesn't make sense to tell her about my crush on her anyway. It'll make things awkward, and she opened up to me about her *situational sexuality.* Hiding in a cold yurt on a reality show isn't the right situation for finding love. And then there's the fact that she called me *a friend.*

I have to stop crushing so hard on Poppy.

She smiles at me and wiggles her toes. "That's a fantastic idea. It's like a camping slumber party."

I chuckle and lick my lips. "A campout with thongs." I laugh.

"If only these thongs were flannel. We'd be toasty warm."

"*Merino wool,* you mean. We are *classy ladies* with *high* standards," I say. And we laugh because our little pile of clothing with the added stolen suitcase means we're wearing the pink thongs tomorrow. *Why didn't the bag have actual garments in it?*

"Wool thongs? Now, that would be cozy glamping. Let's get famous and start a couture Alaskan clothing brand. We'll have merino wool thongs, seal fur corsets—"

"Don't forget the faux fur bikinis," I add, laughing.

Her smile is spontaneous and seductive. Her carefree attitude and easy smile attracted me to her in the first place. I'm happy that we get to spend weeks together in this private yurt for our gameshow adventure. But I know that she isn't looking for love. Her focus is on winning and her future as an elite triathlete.

Poppy's eyes sparkle, reflecting in the lamp light. "Life is full of surprises, isn't it?"

I nod with an overwhelming longing swelling within me. I wish I could tell her how I admire her anything-goes attitude and want more than a friendship. But I'll settle for a slumber-party snuggle, buddy.

The cold breeze intensifies through the yurt, causing us to rearrange our sleeping setup quickly, pushing our bunks together. We pull the blankets over and huddle close. Our shoulders brush, and I enjoy the warmth of her body near me.

"Hey, you think this is cold now?" she says with a smile. "Wait until we're out there surfing on icebergs in bikinis."

"I'm sure tomorrow will be our snow sculpting challenge unless they schedule the Northern Lights for us to use for the dance party challenge."

We break out laughing, our bodies wiggling against each other. We continue chatting, our voices filling the yurt with easy laughs and sharing funny Alaskan challenge ideas. She's hoping for a physical challenge, while I am hoping for a hot chocolate-drinking challenge, my special talent.

We mesh like we've been friends forever, not a mere two days— but they are Alaskan days, stretching from five in the morning until midnight. And add on the intimacy of a near-death experience. I guess we are closer than college roommates but not as close as lovers. . . *yet.*

As the freezing night wears on, our banter gives way to comfortable silence. I steal glances at my warm bunkmate. Her profile is illuminated by the soft glow of the lantern, giving her an ethereal glow. She looks beautiful, and I can't imagine being anywhere else but here next to her.

Thank God our cruise boat sank!

With our casual closeness, I shift on the bunk to lay on my back with our shoulders pressed together. She turns to me, her eyes locking onto mine. For a second, I see something sparkle in her deep brown eyes, mirroring my desire.

The air between us charges with unspoken electricity. Our bodies are pulled closer, with our noses almost touching. Her warm breath tickles my lips, and the world freezes in place. The arctic wind billowing through our yurt, the ridiculous competition, and our stresses disappear with our hot breath mingling as our lips almost touch. A loud rustling outside the yurt shatters the moment.

Startled, I pull away and sit up with my heart pounding-*from our almost-kiss? What was that noise?* I grab the blanket, and she holds the lantern.

"What was that?" she whispers, her eyes wide.

I strain to listen, the wind gusts causing loud, snapping branches, relentless waves crashing into the rocky shore, and metal clanging from something left loose near the crew's RVs. Beyond the eerie background noise, I strain to hear more.

Is there something else out there?

"I'm not sure. It's probably just one of the other bachelorettes going to the outhouse," I say, shrugging.

We exchange a nervous glance, our unspoken desires lingering, but neither of us says anything. The mystery outside our yurt makes us tense and quiet. I stand up, out of our warm bed, ready for whatever is in the wilderness.

The night air is biting, and the yurt creaks without other sounds. The world outside our door is oddly silent, holding its breath with us. As the seconds tick by, the room grows colder and darker.

A sudden foreign rustling outside makes us jump.

I freeze, my eyes wide, and my breath held.

Poppy tenses and grips the lantern like a weapon. "We should look outside," she whispers.

I strain to hear anything, but my fear outweighs my curiosity. "I'm not sure," I reply.

And then, *it* happens.

The yurt's flap opens with a furious rush, and a wild figure bursts inside, her eyes wide with terror. She gasps for breath, her hair tangled and frizzy, her makeup smeared like war paint across her face. She's wearing a lacy nightgown, which looks entirely out of context for the cold night and camping in the woods. She clutches a small, lilac polka dot makeup case in her trembling hand.

For a moment, she is a monstrous apparition—a nightmare conjured from the depths of our fears. The bizarre and terrifying sight paralyzes me, and my heart jumps into my throat.

The lilac makeup bag breaks the spell, and I breathe. A monster wouldn't bring her makeup kit along to kill us.

"They... *they* lied to us!" she gasps, her voice trembling, on the brink of hysteria. "This isn't a dating show. It's a bloody survivalist show! There's no Bachelor! We'll all die here without witnesses." She absentmindedly picks off her almond-shaped, pastel press-on nails as she trembles, staring at us.

My mind struggles to comprehend her words. She's a contestant, but I don't remember her name amidst her disheveled state. The identical, blond, tall, waif-like Bachelorettes blend together with their sun-kissed hair, tanned skin, and glistening swimsuits. It's a catalog of Hollywood sexbot models sharing the same perfect DNA, only distinguishable by the brand of their designer sunglasses and perfume. Also, the Bachelorettes, except for Emily, haven't tried to befriend me, so my mind searches in vain for her name.

I look at Poppy and shrug, biting my lip and wondering if she's a danger. Still gripping the lantern, Poppy exchanges a wide-eyed glance, unsure what to do.

Is The Smoking-Hot Arctic Bachelor really a sinister survival reality show? Is there even prize money to win?

The Bachelorette's disheveled appearance, combined with her frantic demeanor, gives her words an eeriness. Her wild hair and bizarre appearance add to the terrifying situation.

She continues, her voice shaky. "I can't do it anymore. I didn't bring waterproof mascara or body lotion. I'm done with this, and I'm escaping this show! You two should come with me. We can't trust anyone!"

Poppy and I exchange glances again, this time with uncertainty. Her claims are outlandish, but the fear in her eyes is real. The gravity of the situation is pressing down on my chest, and I'm not sure who or what to believe.

I grab Poppy's hand. *I do know who to trust.*

As quickly as she bursts into our yurt, the girl t flees into the dark, gusty night to the distant lights of Seldovia. Her footsteps recede, and her voice echoes, "Get out! Run!. . ."

I am stunned, silent, and clutching Poppy's hand—my mind races to process the whirlwind of events. The reality show we hope will help us regain our summer income may not exist.

I don't know anything beyond what Conner told us. Maybe Emily lied about meeting Burly, and there's no Arctic Bachelor?

Poppy squeezes my hand, and we don't move, unsure what to do.

"What... what just happened?" I finally stammer with a trembling voice.

Her face mirrors mine with wide eyes, tight lips, and rapid blinks. She inhales and says, "I have no idea, but going out in the dark won't help any. We are safe here, and we'll find answers in the morning."

She's a planner, and even though I don't feel safe in the yurt anymore, I don't have a better-*or any other*- plan. I stay quiet.

The Alaskan outdoors is treacherous, even in the daytime. I agree by nodding mutely to her, and we only have a few hours until the sun rises. Staying together in the yurt makes sense in the darkness, especially when we don't know what's happening.

Seconds ago, we were cuddling and laughing—close to kissing. Now, shaking, we crawl into the shared bed, tense, and hold each other out of fear.

Chapter 6

Poppy's Morning Surprise

"*Ring. RIIIng. RinGGG!*"

A bell's clear, high-pitched ring wakes us as the crisp morning is interrupted by the dinner bell suspended from a wooden post near the center of the camp.

"Filming is starting! Wake up time!" Conner calls out sing-songy.

I sit up, my heart pounding with apprehension. Baby stirs beside me and sits up, rubbing her eyes and frowning.

The morning light filters through the fabric of our yurt, casting a soft glow, making the odd night surreal in the daylight. Baby and I huddled together for warmth after the terrifying visit and finally fell asleep from exhaustion.

We hear the contestants rousing, and Conner explaining he has an announcement.

"Let's go see what's happening," Baby says, pulling on her clothes.

I slip into a pink thong, jeans, and a t-shirt to hurry to the middle meeting area and claim a log with Baby. One by one, the other contestants emerge from their yurts, blankets draped over their shoulders and sleep still clinging to their eyes, drawn out by the clanging bell. There are only six other Bachelorettes. The wild-haired one from last night is missing.

Conner and the film crew member who referred to us as *ugly* and *the underdog* stand to make an announcement.

"Good morning, ladies!" Conner greets us cheerfully, and the crew member by his side wears a forced, tired smile resembling my tight expression.

Conner continues, "We just wanted to apologize for last night' unfortunate mishap. We didn't realize cabin fever was real, and Kirsten was suffering from it. Please speak to the medic if anyone else feels their mental health is suffering." He looks at each of us. "Sorry about that. We're here to ensure you have a great experience on the show and find true love."

The consensus among the others' whispers was that she'd never been camping before, and the dark terrified her. She decided to escape to Seldovia's lights and couldn't wait in the terrifying dark until morning.

Despite Conner's attempts at calming us, I'm tense and tired from our crazy night. I exchange a wary glance with Baby, who remains quiet but alert.

He clears his throat, his demeanor shifting to professional, and the filming crew starts, capturing his words. "Today's filming plan is exciting. We want to capture some candid moments of you all meeting and interacting with our Arctic Bachelor, Burly. I know it'll be special and love at first sight for many of you."

I raised an eyebrow at his suggestions for our reactions. The name *Burly* is already questionable, sounding more suited to a pet than a guy. Baby's silence persists, and I nod in response to Conner's announcement.

He continues, "We'll also be setting up a *fun* Arctic challenge for you today, with the winners earning a special date with Burly tonight, so put on your sexiest outfits and *claws out,* girls!"

They wave to us to get prepared, and we slowly get up with the rest of the contestants to get ready for the day. I turn to Baby. "Well, it looks like our plan to win is still on. This is a dating show, after all."

She rubs her hand through her hair and looks around the camp, her eyes not settling on me. "This is ridiculous, Poppy. I can't believe we're continuing. They want us to compete for a date with a rando guy. Sure, the coffee and camp is nice, but it's time we find a way home instead."

I place my hand on her shoulder and give her a warm squeeze. She says she wants to leave but leans into me, and I pull her closer so she can lay her head on my shoulder as we watch the campfire.

"Dating isn't what we want, but we have a good plan. There's a reason we're here. Nothing's changed. Plus, another girl is out, so our chances at winning are *better.*"

Given her current mood, I don't want to push her. But at the same time, we make a great team, and Baby's amazing; any man or woman would be lucky to have her! I know she needs money just as much as me, and having two competing doubles our chances of winning. I'm flying to Australia in a month for a triathlon. I can't qualify for the next competition if I don't compete. I've worked too hard to quit, and Baby needs to finish her degree.

No quitting! We are winning this show, no matter what!

"Come on, Baby. It's just the third day of our slumber party. We got this!" I smile at her, and she meets my eyes and then nods.

"Besides, we have the pink thongs now! How can we lose?"

She giggles, leans further into me, and we watch the fire flicker. "You're right, Poppy. I'll focus on getting through each day, and I'll help look for a way to win."

I hug her, grateful she's staying and enjoying her beside me. Her body fits perfectly next to mine, and her caramel skin mixes well next to mine. I can see our friendship growing into something more after we win this silly game show.

I inhale her scent. *How does she smell like mountains and cinnamon when we use the same stolen pink products?*

"Exactly. And maybe we can make the best of this situation and have fun along the way."

She sits up, licks her lips, and pushes her shoulders back. "All right, Poppy. I'm ready. Let's show them what Alaska women are made of."

"Mostly coffee and blueberry sourdough pancakes, by my estimation," I joke.

She laughs again and opens her mouth but closes it and looks back to the fire. I can't shake the sense that Baby's holding something back.

"I'm going to use the facilities. I'll be right back," I whisper to Baby as we wait for all the bachelorettes to be ready and the film crew to set up.

She nods, her expression still uncertain, and she swats at mosquitos flying around looking for their breakfast. "Sure thing, Poppy. You can take your time." She waves to the contestants in various stages of getting ready, from trying on different hats to applying layers of makeup using the reflection in the RV's side mirrors.

They took away the plugged-in mirror in the coffee area. The crew values hot coffee much more than a lighted mirror-*rightly so!*

I go to the edge of the camp towards the woods and relax in the serene forest. As I enter the dimly lit outhouse, relief washes over me. I'm alone, and it's a welcome break from the constant scrutiny of the film crew and the camp's hustle and bustle. I finish quickly and am about to exit when a voice outside the door makes me gasp.

"Hey there," a deep voice says, "Sorry to startle you," as I open the door to see a man standing outside the outhouse. He's tall, with a fit build, a warm smile, and Polynesian handsomeness, which is out of place but refreshingly yummy in this remote setting.

"Oh, no problem," I reply, my heart racing from the unexpected encounter. "I just needed a moment alone."

He chuckles, his brown eyes crinkling at the corners. "I completely understand. It's pretty chaotic back there with all the cameras and competition."

I frowned slightly, assessing his thick arms straining his surfing shirt. He must be setting up for the filming and hiding for a break.

"Rip Curl. That's a trendy surfing brand. Are you a surfer?"

He gives me a shaka hand sign and laughs. "I guess you mainlanders wouldn't know-that means yes! I surf and am this close," he says as he holds his fingers together, "to being sponsored by Rip Curl."

"Nice!" I smile at his exuberance. "Hey, you're in Alaska now. We call the clueless folks the lower 48ers. Like, *I can't believe these 48ers didn't bring bug spray to a camping trip.*"

He laughs. "Well, they are all from the hills of Hollywood. Conner picked his friends for the show to help them in their modeling and acting careers."

"Ah, that explains the plethora of blondes and the inability to go anywhere without taking two hours to get ready." I shrug and look at his tanned skin and broad shoulders. "Are you a Hollywood friend, too?"

"I'm *friendly,* but do I look like a model or Hollywood type?"

Yes! He looks ready to be cast in the next Aquaman movie. I shrug and lift my eyebrows, not wanting to offend.

"I'm Hawaiian. This is my side hustle before surf season picks up," he explains.

"Okay, hustler. Then can you hustle us ladies up heaters in our yurts? It's seriously cold at night, and you guys are in your battery-powered RVs while we are shivering," I say.

"Sure thing! I'll figure that out for you guys," he winks and me.

"Thanks. I'm Poppy, by the way."

He extends a calloused hand, which I shake firmly.

"Kai. Nice to meet you, Poppy." Kai's easygoing demeanor and the glint of adventure in his eyes make me smile. He's my type of guy, and I could see shooting darts with him at a bar and maybe even attempting surfing.

"You're from Hawaii. Do you know Dig Me Beach? I competed there in the World Ironman, and I loved it!" I exclaim and lean in, touching his arm covered in a dark tribal tattoo.

He nods, his excitement bubbling into his eyes. "Epic waves, and you can't beat Kona coffee. I miss home!"

I lean forward and gesture to the breathtaking mountains and ocean around us. "Alaska has its charms, too. But I wouldn't mind a little sun and sand right about now." I enjoy bumping into Kai and our friendly chatting. He has a hard-to-resist charm. *Making a friend with the filming crew would be to our advantage.*

"Hey, let's talk more later. Okay?" I say, reluctantly excusing myself from our conversation, aware Baby's waiting for me and the competition starts soon.

He gives me a warm smile and a shaka sign. "See ya around, Poppy!"

Returning to camp, the other contestants look camera-ready with their flawless makeup, perfect hair, and fashionable outfits, and a pang of insecurity hits me. Models surround me, and Baby and I are the ones who stand out, *but not in a good way.*

"Today's challenge, you'll work in pairs to collect wood and build the best bonfire. The winning team earns a coveted date with our Arctic Bachelor, Burly. So let's get to it, ladies!" Conner claps his hands, and I shake my head at the contestant's long nails and heels.

They were not expecting an outdoorsy challenge!

Baby and I exchange a determined glance. This challenge plays to our Alaskan strengths, and there's no way we can lose. *We're Alaskans—fire is life here.* We immediately head to the woods to collect firestarters, kindling, and firewood.

"I guess they couldn't find glaciers or wrestle up grizzly bears for today's competition."

She bends down, helping me drag an old log. "That'll be tomorrow when they pre-booked our fishing challenge using only our bras. I'm sure they called ahead to schedule the salmon to swim through the camp's stream at eleven fifteen *exactly.*"

We giggle and throw the log onto our pile.

As the competition is underway, it's clear that the other contestants are out of their element. Aside from avoiding getting dirty or going into the forest to find logs, the mosquitoes are swarming them.

The team nearest to the forest should have the advantage, but they are scavenging beach wood on the rocky shore instead of picking up the abundant branches and downed trees inside the forest.

"I kinda feel sorry for them," Baby says as we watch a contestant limp back to camp with a heel broken off her stylish boot. Her low heels proved challenging to walk with through the woods.

"Poor girl! I want to help, but we are competing. Two of the Bachelorettes have already met Burly from the first challenge. We *need* this alone-time date advantage. There are still six girls left who could take our money." I drop my armload onto our pile, and Baby dumps hers onto mine.

"Jesus!" a contestant says next to us, falling into stinging hogweed by tripping over an exposed root.

It's Quartz, Emily's roommate and the winner of the bear-proofing challenge. I rush over and pull her from the stinging bush. She's covered in scratches, and her skin is angry from the biting bush and mosquitoes.

"It's the worst here," she cries.

"Mosquitos are the state bird," Baby says, "You'll get used to them."

The girl grimaces as red welts spread over her bare legs and arms.

"Do we have a medic?" I call out.

With the camera crew filming, a medic rushes over and opens the first aid kit to start dabbing cream on her.

"Will she be able to continue?" Conner asks the medic as he helps to dab lotion on her legs.

"This is *very serious*. Poison Oak can cause an allergic reaction and kill within minutes," he says gravely, and her eyes widen in fear.

Baby shakes her head.

"Or this is Alaskan hogweed, and she needs to wash off the burning sap," I add, and the camera turns to film me as the medic scowls.

"Either way, she must go to a clinic and can't continue." The medic says, steepling his fingers and looking at the camera instead of his patient.

Is he even a medic, or is this another actor/model friend of Conner's?

Conner winks before the camera lens turns to him, and then he nods at him and helps Quartz stand. "I'm sorry. Your Arctic love journey must end," Conner says dramatically as the contestant whimpers and wipes her nose.

"Our competition is thinning fast," I tell Baby as they carry her off, and we continue stacking wood on our colossal pile.

"Let's take a break and relax for a minute," I say, looking at the scant wood piles from the other contestants. We are moving quickly and efficiently, collecting dry wood for the fire, unlike the soggy and green pieces in the other piles.

Baby nods, and we sit by the campfire, the smoke keeping the bugs away and the heat comforting as we relax into a soft, mossy log.

Before we know it, a cameraman shakes us awake.

"Um, it's time to judge," he says. The camera, on a tripod, is filming us sleeping as the other contestants work behind us building their bonfires.

Damn it!

Baby looks at me and makes a pained face, shaking her head. She whispers, "We hardly slept last night. It's not our fault."

I look at the two other piles. I guess Quartz' partner joined another team. One is larger than ours but with terrible firewood. The second is a tiny pile filled with kindling. The other contestants, disheveled and tired, gather around us. Hair tangled with sticks and leaves, dirty clothing, and exhausted faces, they look nothing like the stunning models that started this challenge.

"Let's light them up and pick the winner!" Conner declares, and the crew coordinates simultaneously, igniting the three piles.

The kindling group's pile burns bright but goes out quickly. The enormous pile is smokey and won't keep the flame alive. Ours is the only bonfire still burning after five minutes.

"Congratulations! Baby and Poppy win the fabulous date with our Bachelor tonight!"

I exchange a smile with Baby. We may look average compared to the glamorous Bachelorettes, but we, Alaskan women, will win every outdoor challenge! *Now, we only need to win Burly's heart.*

The film crew captures our win and the announcement of our prize. Baby and I hug and bow down to the mock cheers of the contestants. Their half-hearted clapping and groaning about bug bites and needing showers complaints are louder than the mumbled congratulations and golf claps.

"If you don't wear perfume, the bugs aren't attracted to you," Baby says quietly to Maddie, the girl complaining the loudest. Bug bites polkadot her like freckles.

"No perfume," she says, her mouth screws up funny, "Then what will I smell like?" She wrinkles her nose.

So much for Baby trying to be helpful. I shrug and stifle a smile at the exchange.

Suddenly, the other contestants start enthusiastically cheering, and my attention is on the man entering the center of camp-*Burly!* Finally, we are meeting the Alaskan Bachelor.

The film crew cordons him off to film his intro before we meet him. The others gather around to watch, blocking my view. I weave around the girls to take a peek, seeing his broad back, posing with an axe in a red flannel shirt, suspenders, and big black boots.

"He just needs a blue ox, right?" I joke to Baby regarding this Paul Bunyan scene.

I don't hear her response because he steals my breath when he turns. *I know him!* I blink in surprise.

He's the Hawaiian crew member Kai, whom I met at the outhouse. Only he wasn't dressed as a lumberjack then.

I should have known they didn't have *a real Alaskan man,* as nothing about this reality show is *authentic!* I suppose even Baby and I aren't *real* since we wandered onto the show, and neither of us is interested in falling in love with an Arctic man or advancing our modeling careers.

I glance at Burly, whose chest stretches the fabric, and his butt is temptingly firm when he bends to grab another piece of log to split for the adorning women and camera. My heart skips a beat, and my cheeks blush when he looks at me and winks.

As the other contestants vie for his attention, I watch from the sidelines, my mind racing. The stakes are getting higher, and the competition for Burly's heart is starting.

If only I had known it was him earlier. Instead of talking about Hawaii and triathlons, I would have flirted and laid on my charm.

The shock of the revelation is still sinking in when Kai—*Burly*—announces he's taking Baby and me on an evening date for a romantic meal atop a glacier.

The other contestants groan, and I'm feeling a little guilty. *Maybe some of them do want to win Burly's heart.* And also, he's a genuinely nice guy.

We have our plan- to win the prize money - but I'm starting to have second thoughts.

"Come on! Let's get ready. I found out there's a costume person who'll dress us. I can't wait to see what they come up with for a glacier dinner." Baby smiles victoriously and gives a jaunty wave and smile to Kai as she pulls me to an RV.

I smile and nod. *I can't disappoint her, and I just finished convincing her to stay.* The prize money is her money, too. I don't want to be why she can't pay for her business grad school.

My competitive instinct is declining by the second. After meeting Burly, Baby looks ready to win, and I'm more prepared to leave.

I should go home and quit this nonsense. Baby was right!

Chapter 7

Baby, Winning the Date

The helicopter lifts us above the breathtaking Alaskan wilderness, and I marvel at the incredible scenery below. Jagged peaks and vast glaciers hidden behind contrast the beautiful ocean we've enjoyed working on this summer. Seeing Alaska from above is breathtaking and as magical as a whale breaching over the deep blue waves beside our cruise boat. Alaska is the prize for this show. The crew and contestants just don't know how lucky they are to be in the middle of this astounding place.

Burly, our handsome prey, leans over, yelling above the chopper's blades, "This place is amazing, yeah?"

Poppy grins, her enthusiasm bubbling to the surface. "It's unreal! I've lived here for years but never seen the mountains and glaciers from a helicopter!"

I nod in agreement, eyes scanning the rugged, untouched landscape below with the deep blue crevices of the glacier brilliantly cracking the white expanse. "It's the opposite of the gorgeous beaches in Hawaii, huh?" I say to Burly.

Poppy shared her surprising encounter with Kai/Burly and his not-so-arctic background as we got ready.

He chuckles and responds with a laid-back surfer gesture, flashing his pinky and thumb and giving us the shaka sign. "Yeah, you got that right. But there's something special about this untouched place, too. It's an unusual, rare, one-of-a-kind beauty." He studies the wilderness and beauty rushing beneath.

I look at Poppy, and I'd describe her in the same terms. She doesn't need make-up or a fussy hairdo to make her natural, indigenous beauty shine. She's something extraordinary, and I think Kai will appreciate that, too.

As we touch down on the glacier, the chill in the air hits us. The stunning backdrop of ice and snow doesn't fully distract me from the cold. And, of course, the wardrobe person dressed me in fleece and mock fur-lined jackets and boots, giving me very little protection from the freezing environment. I shiver and hug myself.

The helicopter ride and glacier are a lovely backdrop for filming, but it isn't exactly ideal for a romantic, *comfortable* dinner.

The crew has set up a makeshift dining spot with a table, chairs, white linens, and candles. It's a valiant effort, but the freezing temperatures make it clear this will be a quick meal. Kai looks hypothermic, shivering and tucking his head closer to his core, like a sea turtle hiding.

Poor Kai!

He hasn't yet acclimated to the Alaskan summer, and now they drop him on a glacier without proper snow gear. *Why didn't they give us a heater or snow suits instead of fine china and expensive crystal glassware?*

"Bon appétit," the chef says, serving our plates with a flourish—Atlantic salmon, California sushi rolls, and baked Alaska. The irony is that none of the ingredients nor dishes are Alaskan.

I suppress a giggle and look at Poppy, who is poking the soft, pale, farmed salmon with her fork.

She looks up and shakes her head in disgust. *Serving farmed salmon is the worst offense imaginable to an Alaskan.*

Poppy leans over. "When I think of authentic Alaskan cuisine, I definitely expect imported farmed salmon." Her voice is dripping with sarcasm.

Kai looks at Poppy's frown. "Are you vegan, too?

I laugh.

"Could they get a meal more wrong?"

The cameras are on us, so I stifle my laugh and pour the champagne.

Poppy fingers the plastic faux fur around her face. "I keep thinking this must be some sorta joke show, like a spoof of being culturally inappropriate. They are choosing the *most* culturally offensive things."

Kai is silent, conserving his body heat.

I nod. "Except we are the only ones who notice. And the other Bachelorettes and the crew are clueless."

"Conner is *trying a*nd means well," Kai chimes in. "Maybe you should tell him what he's doing wrong."

I nod but disagree since the film crew hasn't been receptive to our suggestions so far. I think of the pissed medic when I tried to explain hogweed.

As the cold wind nips at our faces and our breath mists in the frigid air, I realize eating this meal is more challenging than the last challenges the game show threw at us. *How can we eat and impress Burly with our teeth chattering and fingers curled into fists?*

Conner appears and introduces us to the cameras. "Here we have our true Alaskan Bachelorettes, trying to win Burly's heart on this intimate one-of-a-kind romantic dinner on the edge of a glassiere-"

I look at Poppy, and she presses her lips together to not laugh at his attempt at saying glacier.

"—They are enjoying the best Arctic cuisine, and the only thing hotter than that baked Alaska is our Smoking Hot Eligible Bachelor, Burly."

Burly's smile tightens at the description, and he leans forward. "Hey, Conner. Maybe we could use an Alaskan chef next time. You know it'd be more authentic, and using locals plays better to the audience. Don't you think?"

Conner interrupts him. "—You are *absolutely* right and *so culturally sensitive*, which is why we picked you for the Bachelor." He turns to us, "Do you know an Alaskan prayer to say that your ancestors or People say before the meal?"

Poppy looks at me with a fire lit in her eyes like the offensive question is going to push her over the edge, and she is ready to toss these lower 48'ers down the mountain to the freezing ocean below. I look at the grotesque Atlantic salmon—*Murder is justifiable!*

I place my hand on her leg and answer with a smile to the camera. "No. We don't pray without the big dipper to our Northern side. Bad luck."

He nods, and I continue smiling as Poppy and Burly poke around the salmon to eat the vegetable garnish.

I glance at Poppy and the ocean from above, the sun hanging low in the Alaskan sky lighting up this evening. At least the glacier is breathtaking, and the view is stunning. This romantic candlelit meal is only missing the romance and the meal part.

I turn to Kai, about to distract him by asking if he's enjoying Alaska's unique midnight sun, but one look dries up the words in my mouth. His sheer discomfort is apparent, his forced smile not quite reaching his eyes, his rigid cold body, and he is attempting to fluff his scarf around his neck more.

I reach over and help tuck the scarf tighter to keep the chill out.

"Thanks," he says.

The best way to win over our hot but freezing Bachelor is to warm him up and keep him alive. If his teeth chatter anymore, he's going to crack them! So much for talking and getting to know him on this date. He's definitely not in the mood for romance!

"They should've thrown us a hot tub date, right?" I remark.

"Yeah, man. That would've been epic," he says, a smile touching his eyes.

Poppy nods. "Another miscalculation by management, I guess. Maybe they have something hot to drink?"

"We've got blue snow cones if you want that instead." The chef appears, looking at our untouched food.

Really?!

"Do you have hot soup or tea?" Poppy asks, and he shakes his head, rushing back to his heated prep area and leaving us alone with the film crew on the freezing ice block.

Kai tries to make the best of it and smiles. "Well, at least we won't go hungry," he jokes, attempting to handle chopsticks with his frozen fingers.

"No offense, guys," Poppy says to us, then turns to the crew. "How long do we need to be out here?"

The crew looks as uncomfortable as us, stomping their feet and scarves covering their faces. Under his multicolored cashmere scarf, Conner answers, "Long enough to get shots of you guys laughing and flirting. You know. We are selling romance."

Poppy nods and looks at us, asking, "Why did the snowman call his dog 'Frost'?"

Kai looks confused and says, "Why?"

"Because Frost bites!" she says with a wide grin and laugh.

I chuckle, then laugh, understanding the assignment.

Kai winks at me and joins in, laughing and patting Poppy's shoulder. "Good one!"

He says, "Why did the sand blush?" And pauses, adding, "Because the sea-wee'd!"

We laugh harder at this one, and I see Poppy's eyes tearing up.

They look at me expectantly.

I bite my lip, thinking of a joke. "Why don't scientists trust atoms?"

Poppy leans to Kai. "Of course, she tells us a smart joke. She's in graduate school. *A looker, and she has a brain.*" She winks at me.

I smile. "Because they make up everything!"

With this joke, we are so cold and tired that even the crew starts laughing at our over-done responses.

Kai puts his hand over my hand on the table and leans over to say, "Your joke is much funnier than mine."

"Baby wins the joke challenge," Poppy announces.

I cover Kai's icy hand with my warmer hands, not to flirt or for the cameras, but because he's freezing. "We thought you were a rugged Alaskan Arctic Fox."

He lets out a dry laugh. "Trust me, I'm about as far from an Arctic Fox as you can get. I'm just a guy who got roped into this show by a friend."

"You must owe him a big favor to be freezing your balls off here instead of surfing in the Hawaiian sun," Poppy says.

"Something like that," he says with a shrug and a slight blush.

I couldn't help but smile. Maybe Burly wasn't what we anticipated, but there's something sweet about his easy nature and honesty. And he is very handsome, in a strong, Aquaman-sorta-way.

"Can you tell me about the beaches in Hawaii? I need inspiration for my training in these waters—visualizing swimming in the warm Hawaiian waters will motivate me." She leans in, interested in hearing all about the Hawaiian swims and beaches, while I pour a round of champagne.

Her request makes Kai's eyes light up. Talking about the currents and the tides on his favorite surfing beaches are his favorite topics. They bond over his love for surfing and her love of ocean swims. And I enjoy watching them exchange stories and laughter. They have a genuine shared interest, forming a connection between them and making them forget about the cold.

It's clear that Poppy is a better match for Kai than me. They love the ocean, travel, and sports. He leans into her, and it's equally clear he's attracted to her.

Who wouldn't be? She's tall, raven-haired, with full lips, a sparkling smile, and a quick laugh. Watching her and listening to her warm conversation warms me up, too. *Poppy's perfect!*

I sit back, observing with mixed emotions. On the one hand, I'm happy for her. She deserves love and happiness. On the other hand, I can't help but feel guilty for Kai, who is looking for love and falling for our plan to win.

The show is a big lie, presenting Alaska, the contestants, and the Bachelor in a way to attract viewers. Maybe our lies aren't too bad. We are lying out of convenience, after all.

We needed a place to stay and money; they needed ten Bachelorettes, especially "authentic" Alaskan Bachelorettes.

"I need a partner more than I need to be comfortable on a beach, and I wasn't finding love in Hawaii," Kai explains when Poppy asks why he joined the show. He opens up about his search for someone special.

Sitting across from them, I'm the third wheel on their date.

He's not just here for the cameras. He believes in finding love. And it appears he is finding love with Poppy.

I sympathize with him. He is a genuinely good guy, and it's clear he's looking for something real. We're lying to Kai and the game show about our true intentions.

He leans in, his eyes looking deeply into hers. "You know, Poppy, this whole adventure... it's not just about the show for me. I've been searching for something real, a meaningful connection."

Conner is behind Poppy and directs the camera to zoom into Burly's serious face.

She responds, "Oh? What do you mean?"

His voice carries a hint of wistfulness, and the lens focuses on his deep brown eyes, which collect moisture on the edges. "Well, I've been on my share of wild adventures, riding waves, exploring the ocean. But love, that's something I've always felt was missing. And this show, as crazy as it is, feels like my last chance to find it."

"That's... quite a journey you're on, Kai," Poppy says, and Conner clears his throat and glares, mouthing *Burly*.

She repeats, "*Burly,* that's quite the journey. Thank you for sharing it with me."

Why didn't Conner make the Alaskan man, Burly, repeat his lines without the surfing references?

He is obviously not an Alaskan Arctic Man, as they advertised. Maybe the editing crew will cut that part out. That poor editing team will have their work cut out for them, making this inedible, freezing dinner appear like a dream date.

Or maybe not, as I glance at Burly and Poppy, leaning together, his hand covering hers as they laugh.

We planned on winning, and Poppy's got her eye on the prize. Also, she's more suited to him because of their shared interests, and she can love a man or woman. I'll help Poppy to win this competition for us. After all, if she wins the prize money, I get half and can finish grad school.

He says optimistically, "Well, this might not be the most romantic dinner, but at least we can say we had a meal on a glacier, right?"

Poppy nods. Her hands took over Kai's a long time ago, and she continued to hold his hands to warm them. Our meals remained untouched, the cold stealing our appetite. "A memorable experience." She smiles and lets go of his hand to take mine, and we hold each other's hands.

"Pause here!" Conner yells, and we freeze, literally, in place while the camera sweeps the scene and focuses on each of our hands, then our cold, rosy faces.

I smile weakly. "Did we get enough shots to go back and warm up at camp?"

Conner nods. "Good job guys!"

Kai laughs. "How do the locals here survive if even in summer you can freeze to death?"

"We use real fur and drink hot coffee," Poppy says.

Kai chuckles, and his smile grows. "There's the answer. Conner we need fur and coffee when we get back to camp." He winks at Conner.

Conner says, "Cut" to the camera crew and looks at Burly. "We can't do real fur. We'll offend the viewers and PETA."

"We won't offend them, if that's what Alaskans do. We can get fur parkas from real Alaskan indigenous people and share their way of life with the world. It's amazing they can survive and thrive here."

Conner doesn't look enthusiastic but nods, probably not wanting to offend his Arctic Bachelor.

I add, "It is very eye-opening to see an Arctic hunt or even ask them about a garment. The person can tell you exactly the story of the hunt and the making of it. The Elders show so much reverence and respect to the land and animals. I promise it'll make an entertaining story for the show."

Burly nods, agreeing with me.

“Thanks for the suggestion Baby. We have quite a few ideas that aren’t panning out so meeting the local tribe might be good takes to add into the show,” Conner says. “I could get some candid shots of the local tribes and the landscapes, which will boost ratings among men and Alaskans. Do you watch television up here?”

“Come on, let’s go to the helicopter,” Burly says, seeing Poppy’s eye roll and ready to leave the cold scene.

“Okay, pack it up, team. You guys hop on this helicopter. They’ll come back for us,” Conner explains.

As we leave, I’m honestly surprised to enjoy the bizarre meal and meeting Burly. Also, maybe we can help make the show more authentic and showcase Alaska’s real beauty and spirit, breaking Conner and the viewer’s stereotypes.

Kai turns and surprises us. With the cameras off, he hugs us and says, “Thank you.”

I turn and look at Poppy. She smiles and winks at me like we’ve already won.

Our first date was a success!

And as Kai’s tender, warm embrace lingers, *it felt nice to have his powerful arms around me.* His hug seals our connection and shakes my resolve to play the game.

Poppy nods at me and winks again, her eyebrows raised as we hurry back to the helicopter.

Chapter 8

Poppy's New Plan

Amid the breathtaking helicopter ride back over the icy waters of Kachemak Bay, reflecting the pastel cotton candy skies of the sun setting, we return from our glacier date with Burly. A flurry of emotions swirls inside me as the date goes well, but *Burly* is nothing like I imagined the Smoking Hot Arctic Bachelor would be.

Baby and I step from the chopper, and the crisp night distracts me from the chaotic situation in the camp. Approaching our campsite, the bachelorettes rush past me to greet Burly. They are in new outfits and fresh makeup, ready to impress him and attempt to steal him for some private time.

I only count four Bachelorettes. The perfume-wearing Bachelorette, Maddy, misses her chance to flirt with Burly.

The filming crew at camp are scattered; some are filming Burly and Emily, and the other blonde models are gossiping and arguing.

I catch Baby's eyes. "What's going on now?"

"Maybe the Bachelorettes tried to force them to shoot an *authentic* Alaskan bikini catwalk while we were gone?" she jokes.

"More likely they demanded a masseuse and nail technician," I joke back.

Behind us, Burly tries to untangle himself from the contestants, looking longingly toward the campfire. The camp filming crew blocks his route to warmth, asking him questions about his "passionate date with the real Alaskan Bachelorettes" to stir up more drama and cause the girls around him to try harder to win his attention.

"Hey, I hear something in the woods. Does anyone have bear spray?" I shout toward the crowd, causing them to scatter and allowing Kai to escape to his warm RV.

"You're the real hero," Baby says as the worried contestants pick up their bear sticks and bells.

Conner yells from the forest, "I think we are in the clear. I only saw an owl."

Did he go into the woods searching for the supposed bear?

I shake my head at his lack of outdoor safety.

Thankfully, while we were gone, the crew delivered heaters to all our yurts, but with the current *fake* bear scare, everyone huddles together in the middle of camp by the bonfire. With the four other contestants, we sit around with hot chocolate and cookies, which even the gluten-free Bachelorettes eat to calm their nerves.

Sitting by the campfire, we snack and watch the crackling flames casting dancing shadows.

"You know," I begin, whispering, "I think you're perfect for Kai."

Baby's eyebrows shoot up in surprise. "You and Kai have much more in common. He seems to really like *you,* not me. I think you're our best chance at winning this competition."

"He hugged you," I tell her.

"He hugged you too, Silly," she says, shaking her head and raising her hands at me.

"But he gave you the full *five-second I-like-you-alot hug,*" I clarify with a wink, pursing my lips at her.

She sighs and shrugs. "You are athletic, super-hot, and the same sense of humor. And you love the ocean, just like he does. Plus, your happy-go-lucky nature and optimism are same-same. It's already a perfect match and you just met!"

Kai and I did have a little connection, but I saw a bigger connection between her and him when she held his hands to warm them and shared an extra-long hug.

"Baby, I appreciate the credit, but that's not how love works. Opposites attract." I raise an eyebrow and stick out my tongue at her.

"Maybe opposites attract, but I saw the way you guys easily joked and laughed all night," she says, leaning back and lifting her shoulders like she won the battle.

"Joking is easy small talk. You sat comfortably in silence with him, and it takes someone special to be comfortable without words," I say. *Plus, she is squeezably cute in her puffy parka and rosy cheeks!*

She says, "I don't even like men. Burly is nice. You should forget this competition and see if he likes you."

"Stop! The whole thing, even though he was nice to me, was all for the camera. We need to win, and I think he'll pick you." I list off with my fingers, "You're smart, driven, and the nicest person I know."

She leans closer. "You are the one that can win this. You are the hottest Bachelorette here, the planner who makes lemonade from life's lemons. I wouldn't be here-let alone making it out of that boat-without you. I'm lucky to have you."

I look in her eyes. "Baby, you're selling yourself short. You are amazing and will be graduating with a business degree soon. I'm the one who's lucky to have you as a friend."

Her eyes tear up, and I grasp her hand as we watch the fire. There's comfortable silence as we sit. The crackling of the fire is the only sound in the air.

"Okay, fine," I concede with a grin. "Maybe Kai and I have things in common, but that doesn't mean you can't win."

Baby laughs. "Me winning is *you* winning. We are in this together. So let's toast for a win." She lifts her cocoa mug, and I clink my coffee against it.

One of the Bachelorettes—*Kimmy?*—sits next to me and asks loudly, "Don't you want to know what happened to Maddie?"

The girls turn to us with variations of frowns and exasperate eyebrows as if we should have asked immediately.

Before I can ask, Conner appears. "Alright, ladies, gather 'round. We've got another little situation on our hands," he says with a flourish, turning to the camera

"As you battle each other for Burly's heart, the harsh environment is another war you must win!" He breathes out dramatically and clenches his fist to his chest.

"Our gorgeous model, dog rescuer, and kind-hearted soul, Maddie, could no longer stay in this harsh, unforgiving wilderness and chose to leave today before even winning a chance at a date with our Alaskan heart-throb."

Are these actual facts about Maddie, the girl who complained about dirt and wore more perfume than a Clinique salesperson?

"Did she get stung by a wasps?" I ask Kimmy.

"No," she whispers, "It's the smoke and dirt. She couldn't get the campfire smell out of her hair and freaked out while you were gone."

Really? I look at the others to see if they laugh at her joke, but they nod and continue listening to Conner wax on about the perils of Alaska and falling in love.

Baby frowns and shrugs as confused as me.

"She's rushing home to do a *cleanse* and see her *herbalist,*" Emily adds, "she'll be okay, we think."

From the smell of smoke?

Baby shakes her head, and I'm stunned. *How could anyone abandon an opportunity to be in the beautiful wilds of Alaska and a chance to win the cash?*

Conner's voice is firm as he declares that "any further departures may jeopardize the future of the show itself... remain steadfast and committed to this Arctic adventure and to finding your one true love in the Arctic. Roughing it in the wilds is worth it for Burly's rugged heart. If anyone else leaves there may not be enough to continue the game show."

The gravity of his words sinks in. I *will* win. Kai already likes Baby and me. *We have come too far to quit or let this show implode.* The prize money is so close, with only four girls left to compete against Baby and me. I'll need to pivot and change our plan to help the other contestants stay, or else we won't have a prize to win.

Baby leans in, her voice barely above a whisper. "Poppy, maybe it's time we rethink this. We could walk away from this craziness and enjoy the rest of summer together."

I hesitate, torn between my competitive spirit and the idea of leaving with Baby. But determination surges within me as I look around at the camp and the other contestants. Baby and I are Alaskans, and we've read the Director's instructions. We have a *huge* advantage, and we *need* this money.

"Baby, we are going to win!"

She looks at the other Bachelorettes, weighing their probability of tolerating another week in Alaska. She starts, "Poppy, I . . wanted to tell you. . . I love—"

I hold up my hand, stopping her before she gives me another reason to quit. We have this contest and the money in the bag. I *will* win the competition, and Kai's heart to salvage my summer and compete in the upcoming Australian triathlon trials.

Guys are easy. I'll let him talk about himself, and he'll fall in love with his voice. He loves talking about surfing and waves. And I know he wants a surfing deal, so I'll help him look good on camera.

Then Baby and I will split the money, and we'll even stay friends after the show. She can visit me in Juneau, or I can fly to Anchorage and see her while she finishes university.

We could even go on a trip with some of our winnings. We are so lucky. I bet we'd have tons of fun in Vegas.

My mind is firing at possibilities. "I have an idea," I say so quietly that she is on my shoulder to hear me.

I speak louder, "I guess the show ending isn't so bad."

And Baby lifts her head from my shoulder and looks at me sideways, biting her plump bottom lip.

I continue, "Burly did say he already chose the winner – it was love at first sight. No one came close to how glamorous she is, even camping in the woods. She stole his heart so we don't have a chance anyway." I add dramatically, pretending to wipe a tear as I glance toward Burly's RV.

"His heart has chosen, and it's not me."

Baby shakes her head, bites her lip harder, and widens her eyes at my latest strategy.

I wink at her. I know how confident of their good-looks these high-maintenance girls are—*my new plan will work.*

The other Bachelorettes immediately sit taller, batting their lashes and smiling smugly. One fluffs her hair, and another reapplies cherry lip stain. Emily glances at Burly's RV and positions herself closer. And Kimmy adjusts her pushup bra for maximum effect.

I smile as each contestant is so focused on herself, confident that Burly has chosen them. They are no longer thinking about mosquitos or quitting.

Chapter 9

Poppy's Winner's Resolve

Baby watches Conner laughing and handing Burly props as the crew films "Arctic scenes" with the backdrop of the bay and mountains behind him. I'm debating if I should join her and the other contestants, but she spots me and decides for me, coming over to join me for breakfast.

The other contestants crowd into the spot she left, forgetting about breakfast and the early hour. They encourage Burly and laugh along with Conner. Each contestant is confident she's already won and shoves to be beside Burly in front of the cameras.

Conner announces, "You can enjoy breakfast while we shoot some extra Alaskan scenes." But this doesn't disperse the tittering Bachelorettes.

"We are shooting more film for the editing team today, and we have a very special day for all of you," he says, leading them away from Burly's filming to announce the middle of camp.

"Today, there are two chances to win individual dates with Burly. And remember, at any time, he can choose you as his true love and end this journey, so every moment with him counts!" Conner says.

"This morning is a chance to win an afternoon private date and later we have a special challenge. We've arranged with the local Seldovia tribal elders to create an Alaskan art piece reflecting your experience here. Please go have breakfast and rest before the day's competition."

I glance over and see Burly removing his shirt for the filming scenes. No one is leaving this view!

Burly's broad, dark chest and muscular arms make even Conner pause to watch. He displays tribal tattoos criss-crossing his arms and chest as he holds a bundle of rubber salmon in front of himself like tulips. The contestants swoon and sigh as he flexes.

"Another crazy day," I say to Baby as she joins me on the log, watching the scene.

She nods and smiles. "Your plan to distract and give the contestants hope is working. They all seem to think they are Burly's love-at-first sight."

"It's working for now, but it's hard to imagine they have enough lipstick to last another week here." I catch sight of a tattoo as Burly flexes. "Does he have his name tattooed on his inner arm? Not that the viewers would know since Kai looks nothing like Burly," I add.

"I like the tribal markings. He must have a high pain tolerance to get tattoos across his chest, back, and arms." I can't take my eyes off his tattoos and the muscles beneath him. *If surfing gives me that physique, I need to start surfing.*

"The other contestants think those are Alaskan tribal tattoos. And it sorta drives me crazy the misleading and outright lies they are telling about Alaska," she says.

"Hey, at least we are meeting the Seldovia indigenous community today, and that'll give the show and viewers a taste of real Alaskan culture." I smile and watch as he lunges with a fishing pole.

"Looks like you are enjoying his Polynesian culture!" Baby teases, nudging me as I study his butt.

"It's for the competition. I have to act interested," I say. However, I can't deny there's a certain appeal to seeing his broad bare chest as he models with a trout pole, holding the salmon. Alaskan or not, he has a fantastic body. I spot the tattoo again, though, and I cover my mouth, swallowing.

How can my eyes be glued on the rippling muscles of a surfer dude with his name tattooed on himself?

Baby meets my gaze, lifts her brows, and gives me a sideways look. I can't stop from bursting out laughing. *How are we always laughing when we need to stay focused?*

Conner dismisses Burly back to his RV and gathers us around the campfire again for more dramatic announcements.

"As you know, the afternoon's challenge is working with the local indigenous people to create an Alaskan art piece reflecting your experiences competing in the Final Frontier."

Baby chokes, and I elbow her in the ribs.

At least this time, Conner is almost correct—Alaska is *the Last Frontier.*

Working with the local tribe sparks my curiosity, and I glance at Baby, who's smiling at the news. This challenge has the potential to be a unique and meaningful experience and not the fake nonsense this show has been serving up until today.

"At least we will be doing an Alaskan cultural challenge later," she says.

"We will be *winning an Alaskan challenge,*" I corrected her. The odds are getting better with the thinning competition. I am doubling down on my plan to win Burly's favor and claim the prize money.

"We have an exciting challenge for you to beginning the day with so I hope you brought your appetite! This is an authentic Alaskan cuisine challenge to win a private date with Burly with no cameras on your date," Conner announces and winks.

I exchange glances with Baby. Burly hasn't eliminated anyone, as all the Bachelorettes that left eliminated themselves. Private time with him is vital, with so few of us left.

What will this challenge be?

I've been here long enough to know that the show's concept of *authenticity* is at odds with the real thing.

I whisper, "I'm not sure I'm up for eating their version of *authentic Alaskan cuisine*."

She nods in agreement.

The crew reveals a table with the Alaskan dishes, each more bizarre than the last. I scan the offerings, biting my lip in confusion.

"Can you even identify anything here?" Baby asks me.

I grimace and point to a bowl containing a collection of bugs. "I think this is actually taken from a Survivor challenge. I'm no expert on Alaskan cuisine," I say with a wry smile, "but we don't have cockroaches or scorpions in Alaska, unless you go to the zoo."

As we stare bewildered at the food, Conner announces the lineup of *authentic* Alaskan foods. I roll my eyes as he reveals the items so far from reality it's bordering on insulting: fish heads, dried bugs, pickled seagull, beluga liver—*Is that even legal?*— and fisheye soup are a few *delicacies* he rattles off.

Baby whispers, "No. Just no."

I look at the misguided and outlandish table and debate whether I want to participate in this charade while the other contestants step up to the table to sample bites.

Their disgusting and exaggerated reactions to looking at the dishes made me firmer in deciding not to participate in this farce.

Cameras capture every grimace, wince, and gag, making it all feel like a twisted comedy acting class within the reality game show. *The posing with food and a range of emotions pretending to eat it will be a perfect reel for their commercial acting careers.*

Baby locks arms with me, and we sit on the benches, making it clear that neither of us is playing along with this absurd challenge showcasing Alaskan cuisine. *We are Alaskans and won't participate in this disgusting challenge.*

Conner says, "You must already know what these dishes taste like. You don't want to try them to win private time with Burly?"

Baby squeezes my hand, and we shake our heads at the table of horrors. Baby understands how much I want to win but not at the risk of embarrassing my culture and myself for private time with Burly.

The other contestants enjoy the spotlight and pretend to eat the food as they poke at each dish. I watch as they tentatively sample bites of the seagull, which is the least smelly of the spread. Their exaggerated reactions and choking add to the film crew's delight as they cheer them on to eat more and "try the fisheyes!"

Conner motions for us to join.

"Who will win this exhilarating Arctic Challenge? Can anyone stomach this authentic Alaskan cuisine?" he asks the cameras.

As the absurd food challenge unfolds, the atmosphere is a mix of apprehension and showing off for the cameras. The remaining competitors clearly want to make an impression, if not to catch Burly's attention, then for the audience, as they flash smiles, holding up spoonfuls of untouched food and making jokes about "being up to try anything once."

"Let's agree that we want to win, but not to do anything that risks our lives. This screams food poisoning to me," Baby says cautiously.

I nod, "Usually I'd jump in but I'm a texture person and there's way too much fish slime in those dishes."

Baby nods. "He already likes you anyway and there's no way he's sending you home. I might need it though if we don't lose someone today and they decide to do a rose ceremony."

I look at her, her black curls gleaming in the sunlight and her petite form rocking casual clothing despite the dresses and jewelry on the other girls. "You don't need immunity. Burly knows who's real and who is here for the cameras." I gesture at the contestants fluttering their eyelashes and poking the fisheyes with their manicured nails.

Cheers and chanting begin, and with bold bravado, Emily takes a sizable bite of something slimy and unidentifiable grey for the cameras. Before she can chew or swallow, her body turns pale, and her eyes widen. She gags uncontrollably, and I worry she's having an allergic reaction or seizure.

Instead of the medic, the cameras swarm around her, capturing every wince and grimace while Baby steps forward, grabbing water to help her.

"Are you ready to try the next bite?" Conner asks Baby.

The cameras turn to Baby, allowing Emily to vomit without being on film.

"I'm declining the private date," she says. "None of this is even Alaskan cuisine. It'd be different if you had Eskimo ice cream or herring eggs, but this is offensive!"

I agree. Still, Conner could easily kick her off the show, and his face is turning an interesting color of red.

"She's from the city. She's not used to these Alaskan Bush foods," I say, pulling her back from the filming area.

But what about me? I should play along and take a bite.

Looking at the slimy, fishy food makes my stomach clench, but there must be something edible here. I need to win this show for my triathlon career. *What would I do to become an elite athlete? Would I eat a fisheye?*

The show is a means to that end, and I want to win. Yet, the concoctions on display are terrifying, and the sounds of retching from Emily don't encourage me. Part of me wants to take the risk, to show that I'm up for the challenge and strong enough to endure whatever twisted challenge they give us.

As I debate internally, Baby's hand finds mine again. "It isn't worth the risk of food poisoning," she whispers, tightening her grip on my hand.

My heart flutters as her hand holds mine, and a subtle yet electrifying connection sends a rush of warmth up my arm. I steal a quick look at our entwined fingers that feel so comfortable together. The challenge, the cold, and the smell fade into the background- even poor Emily's retching doesn't bother me.

My competitive spirit still burns brightly, but stepping back from the challenge isn't what's igniting my emotions. The dishes on display are indeed terrifying. However, there's something even more unnerving: the raw and unfiltered emotions coursing through me, triggered by Baby's touch.

Her words and hand are for the competition, but I can't reason with my pounding heart and the coursing heat in my body. *My body wants more than a friend and partner in this competition.*

I lift my chin and exhale. She would have told me if Baby wanted something more than a friendship. She is the most honest, friendly, and thoughtful person. I'm a monster thinking about her as more than a friend when I need to focus on winning this challenge for us. I tighten my grip on her hand and look back to the table of horrors.

Before I can say anything to Baby or contemplate taking a bite, Conner and the film crew take center stage.

"Emily wins the private date with Burly!" Conner announces, and Emily smiles, trying not to gag.

Poor girl! She looks greenish from her bite.

The bachelorettes flee the food table's smell and sit back on the logs, looking shell-shocked.

"Alaskans don't really eat that food," Baby says and hands Emily a water.

The camera crew makes noise and rushes to the table to capture a pair of eagles swooping in to devour the culinary delights. At least the food isn't wasted, and the show gets some nice shots of eagles fighting over fisheyes.

As the eagles take center stage, I glance at the table. Even the eagles won't touch most of it.

Thank goodness Baby held me back. The putrid food would have made me sick.

Winning and being a winner is my life, but Baby was looking out for me, and she was right. Kai's picking the ultimate winner, and eating weird meats and fisheyes won't impress him-*he's a vegan!*

By the looks of the winner, Emily may need medical care, which could spell the end of the competition if she leaves.

"You're so brave. You didn't even need to do that since Burly will choose you." I sidle up next to her and Baby, handing her more water. "If you want to leave the competition and give the rest of us a chance, I'd be super-grateful."

My suggestion makes her smile and take a swig of the water. "No. I'm an influencer, and my followers believe in me. I'm winning the Arctic Bachelor for them!" She sashays away in her heeled boots.

"You might have given her too much confidence. What if the next challenge is wrestling a grizzly? She is meeting with Burly for a private date. We better keep our eye on her," Baby says, biting her lip and watching Emily heading to wardrobe and makeup.

"We are not losing the next challenge," I say, pressing my lips together and pushing my sleeves back.

Chapter 10

Poppy's Homemade Disaster

We gather around Seldovia's tribal elders, a group of Aleut, Yup'ik, Alutiiq, and Athabaskan people. Today's challenge is not about physical strength or beauty but about Alaskan traditions and learning from the elders and our environment.

I'm excited because this is an Arctic challenge made for Baby and me to win. Not only are we familiar with Alaskan art, but we are indigenous: Baby is proudly Yup'ik, while I'm part Aleut, but I am unfamiliar with my tribe, as I grew up in touristy Juneau and my parents aren't active tribal members.

I watch Baby smiling and comfortable in the tribal gathering place, surrounded by elders, even while being filmed. She doesn't look like the shy wallflower from our summer tourist job but a confident Alaskan woman in her element with her people. I can't look away, and my cheeks blush at her radiance.

Conner introduces the challenge and the elders with a flourish to the cameras before explaining the details. "Today, we will use the wisdom of Alaska's First People to create a piece of art representing your Arctic journey for love. You will learn traditional methods and get directions from the Elders, but the art must be made solely by you. Today's winner gets to spend the entire afternoon alone with Burly, exploring and enjoying the mountains."

The challenge is clear - I'm creating an Alaskan craft using natural materials that resonate with the cultural spirit of Alaska. Before we begin, the Elders show samples of their traditional art and explain the significance of the pieces and how they collected and used the special Alaskan materials from the oceans, mountains, and woods around Seldovia.

Baby and I listen intently, showing respect and honor to the cultural traditions they are sharing. While Emily, Kimmy, Addy, and Chloe whisper, giggle, and roll their eyes at the long-winded stories the elder shares about the hunt for food, using every part of the walrus, then carving the tusk with the hunting party scene to honor its sacrifice and teach their children to hunt.

"That would make a better ivory bracelet," Kimmy snickers to Emily, who still looks slightly sick after winning this morning's eating challenge.

After their talk, I walked to the bench to examine the art they brought to inspire us. I carefully examine the art pieces displayed, each telling a unique story of Alaska's rich heritage. My fingers traced the intricate patterns carved into the ivory, and I marveled at the delicate craftsmanship of the Aleut masks adorned with feathers. It is more than art; it's a living testament to the traditions of Alaska's First People.

As I immerse myself in these artifacts, Baby joins me, her eyes gleaming with anticipation. We share a silent understanding, an unspoken recognition of the significance of this challenge for us. Today isn't just about winning- it's a chance to honor our ancestors and showcase the real Alaska we love.

The elders watch us with a knowing smile. Their approval is evident in their warm gaze as the other Bachelorettes fight over the shiny glass beads and leather provided.

Conner directs us to gather the materials we need for our creations and to "use our resources wisely." The elders offer guidance, and the camera crew films them sharing their wisdom on sustainably sourcing these materials, emphasizing the importance of respect for the environment.

Baby and I set off with purpose, our hearts and minds aligned with the task at hand. I walk about my surroundings, carefully selecting materials that are unique to this area and speak to me. I collect petrified driftwood from the beach, a clear orange agate, a slick black feather from a raven, and a perfectly circular rock worn smooth by the ancient glaciers.

The other contestants group together, struggling to collect items and joking with each other. Their lack of care about Alaskan traditions and respect for elders is embarrassing. It makes me work even harder to create something reflecting my respect for them and the land.

Seldovia is the most beautiful place I've visited in Alaska, with its mountains, deep blue ocean, endless sky, and untouched wilderness.

I'll make these elders proud and give this unique place the honor it deserves. I clutch my items tight. I look at the odd assortment in my hand-*what can I make from these, though?*

"I'm going to talk with the Elders," I tell Baby, and she nods, a basket of native grasses, bark, and twigs in her arms.

With a twinkle in her eyes, a gentle Aleut Elder beckons me to see my items. She speaks with a soothing cadence, weaving stories of survival, heritage, and the deep connection between the Alaskan people and their environment, as she demonstrates the art of crafting a medicine pouch with an ancient technique of sewing elk leather with sinew fiber and adding decorations of beads, feathers, and drawings onto the bag. The gentle sway of her hands is mesmerizing, and she explains that the items I've collected are spiritually significant, reflecting the land, and belong in a pouch.

I listen eagerly, soaking up her wisdom, and my heart swells, hearing stories of my ancestors. My hands tremble as I begin to create my medicine pouch. The connection to my ancestors is palpable. I infuse my craft with the spirit of the land, my respect for these Peoples, and the wisdom of my ancestors.

As I work, I notice Baby seated nearby, crafting a delicate woven basket. She's a dedicated business student and a lover of numbers. Her meticulous nature perfectly matches the intricate patterns and mathematical precision required for Yup'ik basketry. Her nimble fingers dance with an elder's story of learning to weave from her grandmother.

I marvel at the harmony between her academic pursuits and her indigenous roots. I couldn't have imagined how her culture and university studies are related. I'm in awe of her beautifully intricate basket with greens, browns, and blacks encapsulating the colors of Alaska.

The sun dips low on the horizon, casting a warm, golden glow over the landscape as we work on our creations. Baby and I are engrossed in the process, our creative spirits taking over, while the remaining contestants wander, dismissing the Elder's help.

Conner calls, "Bring your creations up."

We come to the front, each of us is nervous. I proudly hold my medicine pouch for the cameras and recount the stories the Elder told me as we worked together on the bag. I show the items in the bag and explain how they are sacred and passed down to the next generation.

The Elder nods as I talk, and Baby's eyes glisten. However, Conner is unimpressed and yawning, and the filming crew moves to Baby, who showcases her woven basket. Her basket is visually stunning and has the structural integrity for carrying fish, berries, or wood. The intricate patterns and the use of willow bark, grasses, and colors make it a true masterpiece.

When the other Bachelorettes present their creations, I cringe at them. Kimmy, the model/fashion designer, created a moss bikini resembling a swamp creature costume, but it does display her ample cleavage, which the camera focuses on for *way too long.*

Next, Conner and the crew examine Addy's autumn wreath made with twigs and leaves, Martha Stewart-pretty but not Alaskan in the least. Then, they quickly move on to capture Chloe's absurd headpiece made with beads, glue, and glitter – a psychedelic bird's nest.

Where did she get glitter from?

The final Bachelorette, Emily, shares her rudimentary carved wooden dish holding salmonberries. The earlier food challenge must have inspired her.

I glance at Baby sideways, and she bites her plump bottom lip, thinking the same thing as me. *Emily could win this Alaskan cultural challenge.*

Conner smiles and grabs an orange, five-inch-long berry when a black bug wiggles out.

"Woah! I didn't see that coming," he says, dropping the berry in the dirt and pulling his decorative handkerchief square out of his pocket to furiously wipe his hand.

"Sorry!" Emily says, "They're organic, but I guess should have washed them."

Poor girl! Emily's trying hard, winning two challenges, making her our top competition.

I wink at Baby.

Conner looks like he wants to bleach his hand, so we should be safe from her winning. If not for the bugs, Emily's sweet salmonberries might have won him over.

Salmonberries are seriously delicious and an authentic Alaskan sweet treat. I wish I had found them to snack on.

"Baby wins the evening date with Burly," he says, then whispers to the crew, "Does anyone have wet wipes?"

They shake their heads, *no*, and he waves us out of the outdoor tribal workshop, holding his contaminated hand out. "Let's hurry back, Bachelorettes. Baby, you go get ready for an ATV ride and picnic in the wilds of the Alaskan mountains with our Smoking Hot Bachelor."

"I don't want to be in those woods filled with killer Grizzlies anyway," Kimmy whines.

The Elders shake their heads at the scene and Kimmy's comment.

"Good Job, Baby," I say, walking next to her and grabbing her comfortable, perfect hand.

She nods and stops to say goodbye to an Elder.

I add, "Thank you for having us and teaching. I appreciated it." And I smile and nod goodbye to the tribal elder circle.

The camera guy looks at me and asks, "Do you think we will see a grizzly today?'

I look at the camera and give my full Alaskan smile. "Seldovia has *brown bears*, and the salmon aren't in season. So there aren't any bears around. Unfortunately, I don't think you'll see one to film. Although, it's fortunate for us, so we don't have to worry about sleeping outdoors." I wink at the camera and hope they don't cut this clip.

The idea of being terrified of Alaskan bears is ridiculous. Bears don't want to interact with people and aren't blood-thirsty predators.

"Are you going to wrestle a Grizzly for the cameras?" He asks Baby, ignoring my answer.

She gives a sweet grin. "No. I'll let Burly wrestle them while I cheer him on. I bet he'd win that fight."

Getting the hot take they wanted, they stop filming, and I'm alone with Baby.

She places her arm around my back as we walk. "Poppy, I'm so sorry you didn't win. I know how much this challenge meant to you. Your medicine bag was more meaningful and beautiful than my basket."

"It's okay, Baby. Yours is incredible, and you deserve it! You can teach me to weave later. Now, go win a grizzly-wrestling man's heart," I say, putting my arm around her upper back and holding her.

She stops walking and looks at me, pursing her luscious lips. My heart pounds, looking at how wet and soft her lips are. *What would her lips taste like?*

"I will. We're a team, and we're winning this together!" She turns back, striding quickly back to camp.

"Yeah," I say faintly, watching her arms swing wide as she rushes back to meet Burly.

What if she somehow falls for Burly? I know she's not into men, but he's actually quite sweet, like her, and she's becoming very competitive! *We never discussed how far we would go to win.*

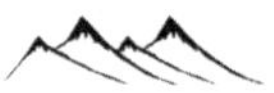

I look up every few seconds and rub my arms, waiting by the fire, waiting for Baby to return.

What if Conner tried to add drama by chasing a brown bear into their picnic?

Or worse, what if Burly kissed her?

My heart races, and logically, I try calming it. *She's my friend, and I can't be jealous when she's not even into men.*

I poke the fire and wait, listening for the sound of a rescue helicopter flying into the woods to save them from a bear attack.

Suddenly, Baby appears, her cheeks rosy and her eyes dancing with excitement as she hugs and sits beside me.

Thank god she made it back! And why are her cheeks so rosy-it's not that cold out here?

"How was the date? Tell me everything," I demand before she catches her breath from bounding over here.

She smiles. "Oh, Poppy, it was amazing! We rode all over the woods and had a picnic at the top of a mountain. I could almost see the camp. I made sure to talk you up. Kai thinks you're wonderful, as you know." She winks at me and grabs my hand in excitement.

My heart swells not by Burly's admiration but by Baby's hand. "Thanks, Baby. You're the best!"

"No problem. We've got this," she says, wrapping her arm around me as we sit in front of the fire.

Burly appears, somehow escaping the filming crew constantly in his shadow. He nods and waves, then walks toward us but is swarmed by the other Bachelorettes before making it two steps.

"Let's go save Kai, and you can say *hello,*" she says, as we notice him trying to escape the crowd, only to be trapped by Emily and a tray of food she's brought him.

Really Emily! He just finished a picnic with Baby. I doubt he's hungry for your snacks or you!

We walk up, and Burly gives me a warm smile while Emily purposely steps to block us.

She says, "We can move into my yurt for some private time. Then you can enjoy my sweet treat without an audience." She winks at him and hands him a cookie frosted with jelly.

"I want a sweet treat, too," Baby jokes, trying to snag a cookie, but Emily moves the tray.

Looks like Emily is upping her game, but she won't win.

Burly takes a bite of the cookie. "Ummm. Good! You want some?" He asks me, ignoring Emily's frown.

I take a jelly cookie but immediately notice the bright berries on top.

"Stop!"

I knock the cookie from Burly's hand, and Baby looks at me wide-eyed as Emily says, "Really, Poppy!"

"These are baneberries!"

"What?" Emily says, her hands on her hips.

Baby's eyes widen in understanding. She asks, "Did you make these?"

"Of course, I did. But *for Burly, not you two!*" She says in a huff.

I look at the tray and the ground and am sure I recognize the berries. *This is real trouble!* I look around for help.

"Are you sure?" Baby asks me, looking at the tray, and Emily is seething, glaring daggers at me.

I nod, my heart racing. The bright red baneberries are easily identifiable and the most toxic Alaskan berry. Eating them causes severe stomach issues and death.

"Stop eating! It's poisonous!" I explain.

The girls around us step back, and Emily shakes her head. The camp quiets, stunned at my words.

Where's the film crew and the medic?

"You're being dramatic!" Emily says with a toss of her long blonde hair.

Baby says, "She's not. Baneberries are deadly. That's what killed the *Into the Wild* guy."

"He's dead?" Chloe asks.

"She wouldn't share with us, anyways," another Bachelorette pipes up.

Burly's brows raise, looking at the cookie on the ground with a big bite taken from it.

Emily pales and suddenly says quietly. "What have I done? I'm so sorry!"

Before Burly can respond, he moans, clutching his stomach, and sprints towards the outhouse.

"Do you think he'll be okay?" Baby looks at me, biting her lip, then rubbing her arm with worry.

I shrug and feel responsible for not noticing Emily's cooking earlier.

Waiting for Baby, I ignored what was happening in camp around me. I could have easily seen Emily collecting berries and cooking with them. *If I had been paying attention, none of this would be happening.*

Instead, I was moping by the fire, worried about Baby.

I exchange a tight glance with Baby, and Emily rushes to find the medic and then leads him to Burly.

Burly's in the outhouse, so the medic questions Emily on how much she ate while waiting for him.

"None! I'm allergic to gluten. And he only had one bite," she says.

"At least no one else ate them. Poor Burly! He's going to hate Alaska after this," Baby says.

I lift my shoulders to loosen the tension and hold Baby's hand. "I hope he's okay. But also, the show won't continue without him."

Emily looks at the medic, her cheeks red. "I think something is wrong."

I look at her, and she's scratching her arm.

"You said you didn't eat any, right?" the medic asks.

I watch in alarm as her condition worsens before our eyes. She lifts her sleeve, and there's a rash spreading rapidly.

"I need to stop the itching!" She frantically rubs both arms, then bends to scratch her legs. She looks like she's been stung by a thousand bees and is intensely itching, with her hands moving and clawing at her neck and chest.

Something is seriously wrong.

"I did taste a little while cooking," she admits, moving to a nearby tree to rub her back against it while she scratches her chest and arms.

I'd laugh at her bear-like behavior if I didn't know how dangerous baneberries are.

I exchange a worried glance with Baby. We may be competitors, but we don't want Emily to suffer.

I'm equally frustrated at myself for not stopping this from happening. *And why didn't the crew and others notice her making this deadly cookie? Couldn't the show have used locals or research before coming here, and we wouldn't be in this situation?*

This is serious and isn't what we signed up for, nor what Emily and Burly signed up for.

Baby and I continue holding hands, the reality of the situation sinking in, and even the other contestants have migrated to check on Emily. The camp is a blizzard of activity, the crew rushing to get her to the hospital and send the medic to tend to Burly. Panic and worry swirl around us.

The medic appears with Burly at his side, his face pale and drawn from the pain, still holding his stomach.

I silently hope for the best but fear the worst with Burly in his RV with the medic, and Emily rushed to the hospital by another crew member.

After twenty minutes, which felt like an eternity, Conner comes to the camp center to make an announcement. His eyes are red-rimmed and puffy.

He must care more than I thought about Emily and Burly!

"Unfortunately, Emily isn't coming back," he says, "But Burly is on the mend. You can't keep an Arctic man sick. He needs a day of rest and fluids. So we won't be filming anything else today, and please only eat what the food cart is serving!"

I nod, and the other contestants sign in relief. The tension dissipates, and Baby squeezes my hand. With the emergency resolved, we all go to the fire, and I forget the competition as we sit, relieved and sharing drinks.

Burly is okay, and the show is going to continue.

"Thank goodness that didn't go bad," I tell Baby.

"The whole thing was crazy, and it was lucky you saw the cookies before anyone had more than a bite." She looks at me, chews her lip, and gives me an easy hug.

I lean in, smelling her fresh hair and enjoying the hug. She's warm and soft.

Breathing in, I remind myself, *Baby is only a friend!*

She smiles, leaning back from the hug. "We're so close to winning. I feel bad for Emily, but as you say, *one less girl*."

I smile and look away from her deep brown eyes.

She continues, "I just wish we didn't have to win by having other contestants almost die. These poor girls didn't know what they were getting into coming to Alaska."

"For sure. The game show is half over. Surely, there can't be any more disasters," I say, poking the fire and letting my heart slow down from her body against mine while we hug.

The Bachelorettes take turns crying on camera about how much they will miss Emily and how worried they are for Burly.

I focus on the competition and say, "Emily was the only one that worried me since she won challenges and spent time with Burly. Kimmy wants to showcase her fashion designs, and Chloe and Addy are models hoping to get contracts from being here. We are going to win that cash!"

"Poppy, I just want everyone to come out of this alive. This game show is a disaster!"

"True. But we're here, and someone will win the money, so it might as well be us. Right?" I say to Baby.

"Right!" She says, looking into my eyes and leaning forward.

I stand up to escape her intoxicating scent and warm brown eyes. I don't want to say something I'll regret. "I'll grab us some more hot chocolate. You want anything else?'

"I do, but it can wait." she takes my hand and pulls me back to the log. "Come on. Let's enjoy the quiet before the film crew comes to tape our reactions to the current drama."

She leans into me, and I watch the fire's flames grow.

Chapter 11

Baby Swimming

The crisp Alaskan afternoon air nips at my skin as I wake up alone, my back pressed against the cold, empty space where Poppy used to be. She decided to sleep separately. We have been cuddling for the past two nights, so this sudden change puzzles me. It's not like we just got the heater last night, or it was colder than usual.

Could it have been something I said or did yesterday when we were both fretting about Burly and the uncertain fate of our ridiculous reality dating show? Or maybe it's the stress of the competition winding down? With only five Bachelorettes left, how much longer can they drag out this charade?

I glance at Poppy's cot, and her hiking boots are missing. She must be off training, probably swimming in the icy ocean. She's adamant about not falling behind in her routine, but even a few days off won't turn her toned body into a couch potato.

I admire her dedication, but I'm also fond of my sleep.

After stretching and deciding to head down to the shoreline, I find Poppy in the water, and my breath catches. She's a force of nature, strong and beautiful. Her muscles move gracefully as she navigates the frigid ocean. She's the real *Smoking Hot Arctic Bachelor;* without fear of the wild or frigid ocean as her lean body, wild hair, and cocoa butter skin cut through the water.

As I watch her tread the smooth ocean and go through her warm-up exercises, I'm in awe. The sun's warm, golden rays paint everything, including her, in a radiant glow, turning her into a sea goddess, the mermaid who rescued me days ago.

The memory of our sinking cruise boat resurfaces and feels like a lifetime ago. So much has happened in just a few days. I vividly recall her taking my arm to protect and guide me through the icy waters. Her strength and confidence dispelled my panic and fear. Back then, I had a childish crush and barely knew her.

Now, we're close friends and partners in this competition. My feelings have evolved significantly. It's not just her beauty captivating me; it's the fantastic person she is, from her easy-going demeanor and jokes to her hidden talents like basket weaving and caring for those around her.

I'm fortunate to be alive and even luckier to have her as a friend. My rebellious mind drifts into fantasies of holding her close, but I quickly squash those thoughts.

We're partners, and complicating things with my emotions wouldn't be wise. We have another week together here in Seldovia, and then we will win the prize. But I'm unsure what will happen to our friendship after this game show ends.

I push those distracting thoughts aside and refocus on Poppy's glistening figure, mentally reviewing our plan to win. Our strategy is solid, especially considering the remaining Bachelorettes and my growing friendship with Burly. We talked yesterday, and I'm almost certain he'll select Poppy to win by the end of next week at the *surprise* Smoking Hot Arctic Bachelor Finale.

I'm privy to the *surprise* finale because Conner, the mastermind organizing the show, has everything planned and scripted. He handed us our scripted parts, instructing us what to say and how to act for the finale scene, standing in front of Burly pleading our case, then crying to the camera after he selects his true love.

I'm *the angry and jilted lover* when Burly picks someone else since we've spent so much time together. The Costume Designer fit me for a hideously silver sparkly dress that is a cross between an alien robot and a runway red carpet look. The six-inch heels alone are pure torture.

Poppy's script has her as *the sensitive and hurt hopeful,* crying and calming herself by gracefully demonstrating yoga poses on the moonlit beach.

I didn't even know she really did yoga.

At the bottom of each script is a note:

If Burly selects you, shed some tears, display excitement, cry again, and then share a slow, staged hug and a fake kiss with Burly for the cameras. Afterward, share a laugh and wave to the camera and contestants as you leave the room alongside Burly while the other Bachelorettes feign disappointment and cry loudly.

DO NOT throw champagne glasses at Burly or the winner per the Legal Department's Request.

The scripted nature of it all is absurd, and my heart aches at the idea of being reduced to such a performance and that none of the other contestants are appalled by this. Even Poppy read her script and is willing to play along.

Of course, we have to play the part for Poppy's dreams and my future, even if it feels utterly wrong.

Amidst my thoughts, a warm feeling creeps inside my chest, thinking about her. A fleeting image intrudes – waking up next to Poppy, her arms wrapped around me, our bodies fitting together, and the dream of a kiss with her.

We're just coworkers and friends in this crazy game show! My cheeks flush at the mere idea, and I mentally shake myself back to our goal – winning the money for our futures. One of us will win Burly's heart to make it happen. I must stay focused on our friendship so our dreams can come true.

As I watch her glisten among the waves, I bite my lip. I will miss her after next week. She's determined and funny. I'm getting used to our nights by the campfire. She's a bundle of joy, spreading happiness to everyone around her. Observing her, I realize how much this new friendship means to me.

While she swims, I have an irresistible pull to join her despite my aversion to the cold. Stepping into the icy water, I peel off my t-shirt and leave on my undergarments. The shocking cold takes my breath away, but I push through it, immersing myself completely.

The frigid water sends an electrifying shock through my body, causing me to let out a startled shriek.

Poppy's laughter reverberates over the water as she swims toward me.

"Hey, stranger," she says, her eyes sparkling with delight.

"This was a good idea when I was warm on shore," I say.

She flashes a playful grin. "I'm glad you decided to join me. It's not too cold, is it?"

"I'm up for the challenge," I say back, my body no longer feeling the cold as I move in the water beside her. *Her confidence must be rubbing off on me.*

"You get used to it," she teases, her eyes sparkling mischievously.

I splash water at her, my lips curved. "I hope so! It's just the initial shock that's a bit . . . bracing."

"No worries. I only stay out for twenty minutes or so. Five minutes more, and we are done," she says, encouraging me.

I scrunch my nose and bite my lip. My heart is racing, and I'm pretty sure I can survive in the Arctic waters for five minutes. "I can't believe you swim out here almost every day."

"It's my secret strategy to win. If I can tolerate the Arctic waters, racing in Australia and Hawaii is a piece of cake," she says, her face aglow talking about competing.

"What if you get a cramp?

"I guess it's a good thing you came out to save me then," she says, teasing me and touching my arm as we float.

"I'll have to add that to my application. Not only am I a wilderness canoe guide and ice carver, but I am an Arctic Ocean lifeguard," I say and swim closer to her to almost touch her and feel her movements through the water.

"Why are you even getting a business degree with all those skills?" she teases back and winks at me.

I look at her wet skin and rosy cheeks, and my chill turns to heat as my insides melt, being so close to her and seeing the passion she has for swimming in the ocean. Water droplets glisten on her skin like diamonds, and the way she looks, the way I feel, I know being friends isn't an option.

We tread water. And silently watch the mountains around us, waking up in the sun as we move through the waves and the beauty of Alaska surrounds us. In this vast ocean, along the wilderness, we're the only two people.

"Baby," she says, her voice soft, "I'm so glad you're here with me."

I swim closer, and our bodies touch.

She automatically puts her arm on mine, and her legs gently brush against mine with every stroke.

"Poppy, I've been wanting to tell you something."

Her gaze meets mine, our eyes inches apart, and our bodies touching with each swirling kick and paddle. "What?" she whispers and leans closer.

I take a deep breath, the cold water sharpening my resolve. "I care about you. More than I've ever cared about anyone. And I thought. . . maybe. . . maybe you feel the same way?"

Her brown eyes crease on the edges, and she gently lifts a hand out of the water to cup my cheek. "Baby, I do care about you. You mean the world to me."

My breath catches in my throat, the weight of her words sinking in. Luck, or being unlucky in our boat sinking, whatever it was, trapping us together in this unconventional situation to reveal our impossible connection.

Before I can find the right words to respond, she leans in, her lips lightly brushing mine in a whisper of a kiss, exploding in heat in the icy Arctic waters.

My heart soars, and I lean in, ready to fully taste her lips and feel her against me. I kiss her deeply, and she holds me while I continue moving in the water against her. Our lips meet in a brief, tender kiss filled with unspoken emotions, a teasing promise of what could be something *new*, something unexpectedly *right*.

As I pull away, our foreheads still touching, a blazing fire spreads through me. The ocean, the wilderness, and the absurdity of our situation created this weirdly perfect set-up for our mindblowing kiss.

She flips to float on her back and gives a carefree laugh. "Well, that'll warm us up for the end of our workout!"

A flash catches my eye on the shore, and I turn. "Seriously?" I muttered under my breath, my cheeks flushing with embarrassment.

She lets out a sigh, her gaze shifting to the shore. She winks at me. "It's as if we signed up for a reality show where there's no privacy, right?"

I smile back at her light-heartedness and paddle with her to the shore.

"If the film crew is awake, then there's hot coffee and breakfast waiting for us," she says while smiling.

"Mmm," is all I can respond, out of breath from the ocean activities.

She gives me a hand out of the water and onto the beach where we had piled our discarded clothing.

"Baby," she says, "thank you for being here with me."

I smile. My heart is still racing. "Of course, Poppy. There's no place I'd rather be."

Conner, Burly, and the film crew watch us yards away at the rocky shore marking the border of our camp and the beach. We pull on our clothes as they talk and joke around like friends, not like the creeps who are filming us.

Reality washes over me. They aren't filming me, but Poppy, who is radiant with her swimsuit clinging to her athletic form. There's no way Burly can see her like this and not fall instantly in love with her.

I feel a sharp pang of jealousy.

"We better head back and warm up," Poppy says, striding away without mentioning anything about our tender moment.

With a heavy heart, I follow Poppy and approach the film crew. I give them a jaunty wave, and they smile in return. The brisk Alaskan breeze rustles the grasses around us, and my cheeks are flushed with embarrassment at an audience for our first kiss.

"Hey, guys," I say, "Listen, I don't mean to be a buzzkill, but you wouldn't happen to have caught any of that on film, would you?"

With a grin, Conner turns to me, an amused glint in his eyes. "Oh, don't worry, Baby. We got tons of great shots of you swimming."

I didn't anticipate them filming us; missing my swim on film isn't my worry. I don't want to broadcast our intimate moment, nor should they with their hetero-cis-gendered dating show.

Uneasiness replaces my earlier happiness as I imagine strangers worldwide watching our intimate kiss.

Kai adds, "Yeah, seeing you two in the water is amazing. The connection between Poppy and you is just. . . incredible."

My cheeks burn brighter, and I look out, wondering how far the cameras can focus and which way we were facing. I steal a glance at Poppy. She's unfazed by their comments, ready to get coffee.

Does Kai know that I like Poppy in more than a friendly way? My kiss could ruin Poppy's plan to win, especially if they show it.

"Is it?" I manage to mumble.

Poppy chirps, "It was a great swim. Next time, you should join us. Cold water swims are super good for you."

"Hey, guys, seriously," I try again, "is there any way you can cut that footage? It's just. . . personal and not related to the show."

Conner exchanges a look with the film crew. He says, "Baby, we're here to capture real Alaskan moments and everything around us. We can't just stop filming when people aren't wearing makeup or feeling pretty."

What!

Kai looks at his feet, wearing his shoes with no socks, and he kicks a rock. He's not saying anything or taking sides.

My hope fades, and I turn to Poppy, silently pleading for her support. But she's looking to camp, her expression calm.

"Don't worry about it, Baby," she reassures me. "We were little black blobs in the big ocean from this view."

Kai interrupts, "I forgot, I grabbed you both hot coffee." He hands us mugs, and she smiles at him gratefully, her hand lingering on his as she takes the cup. Their eyes meet, and they share a smile.

Conner glances at them with a frown.

I don't think Poppy is part of his finale master plan.

She deserves to win, and Kai likes her-He brought her coffee and is here watching her swim.

I take my coffee and walk after her to camp, mentally preparing for the upcoming day and the potential disasters awaiting us.

Walking away, I overhear Kai speaking in a low tone. "Conner, I've decided—I found my true love. Do you want to wrap up this filming sooner rather than later? We could move to a hotel and enjoy Alaska in comfort."

I don't see or hear a response from Conner, but my heart leaps in my throat with a mixture of emotions. I'm thrilled Kai is picking Poppy per *our master plan,* but reality sinks in.

If Kai finds his true love, the game show is finished, and my summer adventure ends.

My mind is in turmoil. My feelings for Poppy are undeniable, and I want to tell her exactly how I feel. But I want her to achieve her dreams, and she is so close to winning the prize. It's a complicated situation, and my feelings overwhelm my rational brain.

I should be happy, but I'm feeling withdrawn and small.

Maybe a cup of hot chocolate and sitting by the fire alone will help?

Chapter 12

Baby's Confessions!

An ice rose?!

The icy rose petals shimmer under the bright filming lights, casting delicate rainbows as the rose drips onto its golden stand and then puddles on the red carpet.

Conner explains to the cameras, "The Arctic rose represents rare beauty and Arctic love. This delicate flower is the selected symbol for The Bachelor to hand his true love, the winner of The Smoking Hot Arctic Bachelor."

But the melting, misshapen rose, like so many of the show's ludicrous ideas, is a flop and does nothing to showcase Alaska or true love. I'm sure an ice rose was a genius idea in a California studio. In reality, it's puddling and becoming unrecognizable.

"We are filming this scene, and we will do some Alaskan landscape shots for the Editing Team. I need all of you happy, socializing, and roasting s'mores on the fire directly after this," Conner pauses and outlines for us.

"In our gowns?" Chloe asks.

"Yes! You need to look stunning. I heard there might be northern lights tonight," he responds.

I cannot sit in this silver monstrosity of a dress, so making s'more standing in six-inch heels will be entertaining. *Does the director want one of us to fall into the campfire?*

With the recent food poisoning disaster and Emily's departure, Conner announced the finale was tonight, and the show ended *today.* I had my suspicions after hearing Burly's whispers this morning.

The announcement is unexpected *but expected. Besides, what other challenges were they planning with the ridiculous list I saw? And how many more Bachelorettes were going to get injured?*

Cabin Fever Princess was right- *We are on a survivalist show, and I'm almost the last girl standing.*

The remaining contestants agreed with the sped-up timeline and were ready to get out of the woods back into civilization.

Addy says, "I'm winning the finale tonight. I was Conner's first high school sweetheart. He owes me!"

What? Is that Conner's plan? He's picked the winner, and Burly will follow the script. The makeup artist is adding another layer of mascara to Poppy, which means I can't ask her if she heard Addy's remark.

I shake my head as the film crew takes wide and focused shots of the rose and the rocky beach stage set up while we patiently wait in our itchy, tight gowns for the Rose Ceremony to start.

"Do you like my gown?" Kimmy K asks Chloe, fingering her neon orange, fringed dress. "I designed it."

I bite my lip, holding back my opinion. *I'm sure there's a particular person who will enjoy wearing that gown. It's just not any person I've ever met.* Until now, that is.

Kimmy K is elated, strutting in it and posing for the camera.

I smile and give her a thumbs-up. *Good for her for taking the opportunity to show off her designs.*

The makeup artist tries to reapply my lipstick, but I wave her away.

Per Conner's instructions for the dramatic individual interview, we should, *through tears,* explain how taxing this competition has been, how much we love Burly, and then explain why we deserve to win. So I'm trying to rehearse what I will say in my head, and it's blank. I can't think of any reason Burly should choose me. I'm not in the top three cutest Bachelorettes here and will not profess my love for him.

My anticipation and nerves about the finale have grown as we wait for Burly to enter and for the game show to choose the winner. Of course, with the chaos of Conner's announcement this morning, I haven't had a chance to talk to Poppy alone about our kiss, which makes me even more nervous. *If it meant something to her, she would have said something to me by now.*

"Keep the camera rolling, and we will let the Editing Team splice and dice it when we get back. Better too much film than not enough for them," Conner tells the crew.

"Burly, we are ready for your entrance," He calls out, which makes us quiet, and we watch him walking onto the beach in his dark suit and tousled dark hair.

Burly walks to the podium and picks up the rose.

The dripping blob's stem breaks, shattering the rose into ice pieces on the red-carpeted forest. Burly laughs and winks at Conner, who covers his face with his hand as he wipes his damp hand on his suit pants.

"Should I try that again?"

Conner frowns but then smiles at the mini-disaster and Burly's laugh. "No, leave it. People, what do we have to replace the rose—to hand to the lucky Bachelorette?" He shouts the question to the crew.

The wardrobe person quickly appears and hands him a clear crystal crown to crown the winner. She also indelicately rips two glittery tiaras off surprised contestants and pins their hair back into place. They've been de-crowned to be ready to receive the special Bachelor's crown.

"Perfect!" Conner sets the crown on the gold stand, nods at Burly to continue, and flashes a smile to the camera. "This is the finale you've all been waiting for. Burly, our Smoking Hot Arctic Fox and Alaskan Wilderness Man, will reveal his true love. He took a risk and dated in the wilds of Alaska to find his soulmate. Our beautiful Bachelorettes competed in unique challenges and survived this harsh Arctic environment to win his love, and tonight you will find out which lovely Bachelorette has triumphed. . ."

As he drones on in detail about the challenges and each of us, I look at Poppy in her elegant blue mermaid gown next to me. The gown perfectly fits her body and appears to be made for her. I don't think it's a coincidence that she is in the most gorgeous dress, and it matches Burley's suit. I raise my brow at her, and she blows a kiss back at me, making me blush.

". . . charmed him with her wilderness know-how . . ." Conner describes me. The camera turns to pan over my silver fluffy cocktail dress, exactly when I was moving my hand to hold Poppy's.

I freeze, and Poppy takes my hand with a smile to the camera as if she's holding it for luck as we wait for the announcement.

". . .somehow each has survived this frozen landscape to win the heart of The Smoking Hot Arctic Bachelor." The producer announces as the camera slowly pans over us, lined up in front of Burly, staring intently at the crown, not making eye contact.

The atmosphere is electric. We all look glamorous, even with our bruises, scrapes, and mosquito bites. Collectively, we hold our breath, awaiting Burly to announce a name.

Poppy and I exchange glances and squeeze each other's hands.

"The moment we have all been waiting for has finally arrived. Burly, please step forward and tell us who you choose to wear your Arctic crown signifying your love for them. Who is your one true love?"

The ice rose is reduced to wet spots on the carpet, and the crown is in Burly's hands. The lighting makes him appear even more muscular and handsome than usual *if you like that sorta tall-dark-and handsome-type.*

I look at Poppy, her eyes glimmer at his tan skin, and the suit stretched over his broad shoulders and chest.

Burly reads the lines on a paper held over the camera. "Ladies, this journey has been nothing short of incredible. I've had the chance to get to know each of you, and you are all incredible in your own ways. I'd like to continue to spend time and get to know each of you, but someone has captured my heart from the start, and our feelings have only grown throughout this time here in the Arctic. The time has come for me to make a choice, to crown my true love—"

The following line on the card simply reads, *Long pause—Say a Name.*

"Don't leave us hanging. Tell us the name of this amazing woman," Conner prods but points to the word *pause.*

"—My true love, the one who melted my Arctic heart—" Burly says with Conner nodding.

My heart races as I turn to Poppy, ready to congratulate her. She is glowing and twirling a strand of dark hair in her fingers.

Heck, she's so beautiful right now. I want to get down on one knee, give her a crown, and propose.

I'm happy for Poppy. I can see her and Kai hitting it off, swimming in the warm Hawaiian ocean together. After all, she deserves to win; here's someone who matches her optimism and enthusiasm. Her *situational sexuality* fits this perfect situation. This isn't about me, my feelings, and our kiss. This moment is about Poppy and her future. Burly and her deserve happiness and their dreams to come true!

As the crew films us in front of the red carpet, Kai holding a crown, I wait, holding Poppy's hand tight.

She squeezes it with a reassuring smile. The cameras capture our expectant faces, and I smile, though I will miss our little yurt and hot chocolates by the fire. The prize money will make this game show worth it, though.

"Baby!"

The world stands still, and no one makes a sound. Poppy squeezes my hand, and I turn to Burly, my eyes wide.

"What? Me?"

I must have misheard him.

Poppy whispers, "Go! Get the crown. You won, Baby!" And she releases my hand, leaving it cold and alone.

I don't move, and Conner steps, taking my hand to congratulate me and lead me in front of the cameras and Burly.

Burly holds out his hand and pulls me closer with his eyes locked onto mine. His brown eyes are warm. "Yes, Baby. From the moment I met you, there was an undeniable connection, a spark I couldn't ignore. You've shown me kindness and compassion, and you are the honest, genuine person that I fell in love with."

I shake my head, unable to talk or correct his *obvious* mistake.

He continues, "Last night, we raced through the woods on ATVs and opened up to each other. Your grace and caring made me love you more. You've never thrown yourself at me or pretended to be someone you aren't. I admire that about you. Also, your intelligence and drive to finish your business degree is exceptional. What can I say- I like smart, driven women!"

He laughs, and everybody but Conner and I laugh with him. The crew sprays us with a glitter gun, immediately making me blink and sneeze.

I look at Conner, shaking his head, wordless at Burly.

Both Conner and I know Burly picked the wrong Bachelorette-Poppy is the driven, gorgeous woman he's supposed to pick.

My mind reels.

"Baby, will you accept my crown and embark on this journey with me?" He gestures for me to bend to accept his crown.

I look at the carpet's wet spots, and everyone's eyes are on me.

"No," I say reflexively and step away. "I can't." I look into his kind eyes, hoping he can see that it's not him but *me.*

I don't love him and can't pretend to be in love with him in front of the cameras and Poppy. I won't profess my love when I'm in love with the girl standing behind me.

The crew doesn't hear me, lost in their world of perfect shots and orchestrated romance. And so, amid their obliviousness, I find cameras moving in and forcing me closer to Burly, my face inches away from his.

His smile falters, and his brows furrow in confusion. The disappointment in his eyes is evident. I keep ahold of his hand but bite my lip.

"Kai," I murmured, my voice barely audible. "I can't do this. I can't accept the crown."

I look back to Poppy, whose mouth is open in surprise. I've never seen anything surprise her, even when we were on a sinking boat. *I can't do this, even if I disappoint her.*

"Baby-" he starts.

I stop him with a steady voice. "My name isn't Baby. It's Bailey. And I'm in love with someone else."

Conner is shaking his head behind the cameras and gripping his notepad.

Kai's puzzled expression only deepens. With a soft sigh, I take a deep breath, my heart pounding loudly. It's now or never.

I take both of his hands and the crown. I look into his eyes sincerely and explain, "I never expected to win. I'm a lesbian."

Kai's weighty silence turns into a genuine, easy laugh. With a gentle smile, he cups my cheek, his touch feather–light. "Of course you are. You can't hide it."

I shrug out of his hand. "But then, why would you pick me?"

"Because I found love here, But the show only allows me to choose a Bachelorette as the winner."

I look around, and I'm the one furrowing my brows. There are only Bachelorettes here. *What's going on?*

As the confessions settle between us, he leans in and presses a light kiss to my lips. It's a kiss of shared camaraderie in the face of these unexpected circumstances. "I never expected to meet a real person here who is as authentic and sweet as you, Baby," he whispers against my lips, his words gentle.

"Thank God—A kiss!" Conner says. "Now crown our *underdog* so we can wrap this up," he barks.

I don't have to say *No* this time as Kai speaks up.

"No!"

Conner throws down his clipboard, "Why?"

"Conner, I love you," he says to a stunned Conner and the frozen crew.

The revelation spurs action. Poppy steps forward, taking my hand, as Kai turns to Conner and takes his hands.

I hold Poppy's hands as we watch Conner's blue eyes mist, looking into Kai's glowing eyes.

"Stop filming. We're cutting that last line," he says, not looking away from Kai's unblinking eyes.

The crew steps back but keeps filming.

"Conner, I. Love. You," Kai says again slowly and leans forward, their noses touching.

"Kai, I love you too. That's why I invited you here. You're incredible. I know you'll get surfing sponsorships when the world sees you like I do," he says to him.

Kai wraps him in a hug. "Conner, this show - your work is incredible. I want you to succeed, too. What do you need me to do?"

We step back to watch the surprising ending as the crew films and the other Bachelorettes stare, their eyes wide and unable to talk.

"This-" Conner leans forward and tenderly kisses Kai, and we cheer at their sweet kiss.

The warmth of their kiss lingers in the crisp Alaskan air, and we are all smiling, watching the surprising finale scene.

Conner clears his throat. "Well, I guess that's a wrap, folks," he announces to the crew. "We'll need to give all this to the Editing Team. They'll make it work somehow."

"About all that. . . I'm sorry I didn't accept the crown," I say to Burly.

He shrugs and smiles, "It's all good."

While I'm making apologies, I turn to Poppy. "I'm also sorry about my name. I should have corrected you a lot sooner, but the longer you called me Baby, the more I liked it, and then I felt silly to tell you my name."

She grabs my hands and laughs. "I know your name. I called you Baby because it fits. You smiled when I said it, so I thought you liked the nickname."

"Oh, my gosh," I laugh, relieved. "I do like it."

"Come on," she says softly. "Let's get out of these dresses and make those s'mores."

Together, we walk away from the cameras, the crew, and the other contestants, popping open the champagne and starting the after-party.

After changing into comfy clothes, we roast marshmallows and joke about returning or burning the stolen thongs. As we sit together, the sun dips below the horizon, casting a warm, golden glow over the Alaskan bay and our little circle of yurts.

Poppy swallows and hands me a gooey, warm s'more. She whispers, "Baby, I love you."

Kai hears and lets out a cheer. "At last!" He smiles, walking up behind us, and I see the camera crew following despite the wrap.

"Kai, if I didn't like you, I'd kill you for ruining this moment," I say, then turn back to Poppy. Her words leave me grinning like a jack o'lantern. My heart swells with joy, and tears prick my eyes. "I love you, too!"

Filming be damned!

I reach out, my sparkly nails, and I gently touch her cheek, and then, without hesitation, my lips meet hers in a slow kiss, sending a surge of warmth through our bodies and a cheer from our film crew audience.

"You Creepers! Find someone else to film," Poppy says, then kisses me again harder.

A giggle escapes as we part, with Conner and Kai grinning at us.

"I better not be dreaming," I whisper to Poppy.

She smiles back. "If you are, you'll wake up in the yurt with me, and you can turn over and tell me you love me again."

We hug and laugh.

"This is supposed to be a reality dating show, not some sweet real-life romance!" Conner says.

"Hey, you've found your special ending," Kai says, but I ignore them and kiss Poppy again.

EPILOGUE: Baby, One Year Later

In the wake of our whirlwind journey on The Arctic Bachelor, life unfolds like a captivating romance movie set against the breathtaking backdrop of Seldovia, Alaska. Days melt into weeks and weeks into months as our love story deepens and evolves.

I immersed myself in my new hobby of basket weaving alongside the Elders, simultaneously putting the finishing touches on my online grad school classes. And, of course, I wholeheartedly support Poppy's dream of becoming an elite athlete—although the idea of plunging into the frigid ocean with her still sends shivers down my spine.

"Who would have thought we'd end up here, Baby? In this beautiful place, where it all started?" Poppy's voice is brimming with happiness as she deftly packs her suitcase.

"Life is full of surprises, isn't it?" I say with a grin.

"Did you pack our sunscreen?" she asks, a playful glint in her eyes.

"Yes, and I tucked away some smoked salmon and salmonberry jam for the guys," I reply, zipping our bags.

My cell phone chimes on cue, and Kai's name flashes on the screen.

His laughter echoes through the phone, followed by Conner's cheerful voice in the background.

"Wait, I'm putting you on speaker, too," I say, clicking the speakerphone option.

"I'm all set for the Ironman race. Are you ready for me?" Poppy chimes in, her excitement palpable.

"We are!" they respond in unison. Kai returned to the Big Island of Hawaii with Conner accompanying him.

"But we didn't call about that. Have you seen the ratings for our *Arctic Love Adventure*?" Conner's voice crackles with enthusiasm.

Poppy shoots me a questioning look, curiosity written on her face.

"I turned off our phones because they were dinging with alerts all night," I admit with a shrug. "I didn't want anything to distract you from preparing for your Ironman."

"We're blowing up!" Conner exclaims.

"That's fantastic! I'm thrilled the show's a hit," I reply.

"You guys were the real stars," Kai adds. "Take a look at your socials."

An alert he tags me in pops up on the screen, and I pause to open it.

"I love Poppy and Baby! They should host another dating show in a sunny locale," Kim Kardashian announces on her page.

"Whoa! That's super-crazy!" Poppy says.

"This is going to be bigger than we expected," I say, looking at her.

"Hey, I'm ready to direct it. Keep me in mind when you're offered a million-dollar sequel," Conner says.

Kai adds, "This time lets do it in Hawaii. No more eating fisheyes on glaciers!"

"It'll be our *Tropical Love Adventure* with only bisexual, situational sexual contestants," Poppy laughs.

I put my arm around her. "I love it," I chime in, excitement bubbling.

"Hey, first you need to get your butts on a plane and see us!" Conner says.

"Yeah. We are ready to cheer for you when you win your triathlon! I even made us *Go Poppy* t-shirts to wear," Kai says.

"Ahhhh! Thanks guys!" Poppy says with her arm around me.

I look into her sparkling eyes, and my heart fills. She's the most adventurous and caring person I know. I'm so happy to have her as my partner and be going to Hawaii with her.

I laugh and say a quick goodbye, looking at the clock.

We must catch our ferry, and I have a Go Poppy t-shirt to wear with my friends when we get there.

I turn to Poppy, a question in my eyes, as I bite my lower lip. "What do you think, Poppy? Are you up for another adventure?"

Her eyes sparkle. "You know it, Baby!"

If you loved Poppy and Baby's sapphic adventure, then you'll love Maria and Captain Jackie in *Wilderness Rescue: Stormy Hearts.* Available now at HarmonyNoble.com.

Keep reading to enjoy the next book.

Wilderness Rescue: Stormy Hearts
Chapter 1: Maria

"COLE!"

I shout into the gusting wind, and just as I open my mouth, a wave crashes against the boat, filling my mouth with saltwater. Spitting and wiping my lips on my cold, bare arm, I can't get rid of the bitter taste from the violent sea and toxic fear crashing over me.

No! This cannot be happening! How can a few hours transform the happiest day of my life to the worst day?

I was on a leisurely boating trip in Kachemak Bay, just outside my new hometown of Homer, Alaska. We were celebrating six months of marriage and a new chapter of our lives.

Cole was teaching me about boating, his passion, and business on the calm ocean while I enjoyed his enthusiasm in showing me how to steer. I watched the harbor disappear as the minutes turned to hours on our Alaskan adventure.

Cole's so busy with the family ferry business, the Homer Harbor Hopper, that this boating lesson is one of our few intimate moments. Although I'm excited to learn about operating a boat, I'm more excited to share the news with him that we are starting our own family soon. I waited on the swaying boat for the perfect opportunity to tell him.

I lost my family at a young age, and Cole is an only child. His parents had him at an older age, and they died years ago, which is something we share: missing family.

Hence, being pregnant is a pretty big deal for both of us. Our dream!

We want a big family and children running around, learning to sail on the ocean, and taking over the family business. Then we can happily retire in our big house overlooking the beautiful bay and wait for our grandchildren.

Of course, Cole's boating lesson and the good news on the tip of my tongue was my carefree life *before the murderous storm and a rogue wave knocked Cole overboard.* One moment, he was checking the sputtering engine to motor us out of the grey clouds rolling in. The next, he was no longer leaning over the railing. The waves swallowed his bright life jacket before I realized what was happening.

I stood there, frozen and helpless.

I shake my head. *I should have done something, then!*

The rain and wind hit my cheeks, wet and numb with tears, the ocean and the foul weather. My hands tremble as I clutch the side of our large boat. It seamlessly glided over the smooth waters when Cole was at the wheel, but the boat is tossed relentlessly in the dark, unforgiving bay without him. The waves batter it, leaving me wet. My cute summer dress is heavier than the weighty gold and diamond jewelry on my neck and wrists. The jaunty boating lesson transformed into a raging crisis.

I wrap my arms around my growing belly and grab the side of the boat, bracing for the next crashing wave threatening to flip it. My feet are numb with the water rising and sloshing on the deck over my sandals. Instead of enjoying my first outing to celebrate our marriage and the start of our family-*I'm left alone, stranded!*

"Cole!" I yell into the gray night. The deafening wind snatches my words and responds by throwing icy water at me. I continue clinging to the side of the boat. My voice is lost in the howling, furious storm.

"Cole! Cole! Where are you?" I cry out. The boat shudders with the relentless assault, and panic claws at my chest while I struggle to keep my footing on the slippery deck.

The Alaskan afternoon is turning dark and ominous with the storm closing in.

Terror surges through my veins. Never in my worst nightmares would I imagine myself in this situation. I stop yelling to rest my raw throat and shield my eyes from the ocean spray to search the dark water for any sign of Cole-*anything*!

There's only the miles of ocean with no land or boats in sight.

I try pushing away the suffocating panic. My jaw tightens with fear, and despite the water dripping off my face, I cough, swallowing the dry lump in my throat.

I fumble blindly for the radio in the dusky light as my slippery fingers search.

My numb fingers touch the hard edge of the radio. My cold fingers can't grip or make sense of the buttons in the cold, with my fear overshadowing my mind.

I can't keep searching and yelling into the storm. I need help!

With the device firmly in my grasp, I twist the knobs with frantic desperation, hoping it'll do something and send a signal to find someone—*anyone to help find Cole.*

"Help, HELP! Anyone? I need help!" I shout into the receiver with my wavering voice, but the storm's furies louder than my pleas, and there's no sound coming through the radio.

In frustration, I toss it aside.

It's just another thing I don't know how to operate. I can't start the motor. I can't call for help. It's hopeless!

Cole is gone. Even if I spot him, he'll be frozen after being in the water this long. And the only way he couldn't swim back to the boat were if he was knocked unconscious.

Will I be able to pull him over the rail and back into the boat? Has it been minutes or hours since he fell overboard?

Time stopped. I look at the swirling, angry ocean and try to determine where the current would have pulled him.

I can't drive the boat. I don't know how to get to shore. Honestly, I don't even know which direction the harbor is. *I'm useless!*

I'm frozen, clutching the rail, overwhelmed as the darkness and chaos erupt around me. I peer over the rail, looking at white-capped waves, but they offer no clue of Cole's whereabouts. My tears are the only warmth as I shout his name over and over, my voice edged with desperation.

"Cole-COLE-Cole Cole Cooooole!"

I grip the rocking boat, my voice cracking—the relentless wind and rain punch me, blurring my vision, and saltwater is all I taste and smell. The futility suffocates me.

I lost everything and everyone when he vanished. No one is left to save me—Cole is my only family.

I'm finished!

The boat bucks and lurches on the raging sea.

"Where are you? How could you leave me here?!" I whisper with a whimper into the abyss.

Each wave crashing over the boat threatens to wash me into the ocean with him.

Maybe I should let go and let the ocean take me?

Sudden lightning shooting through the dark sky flashes against my colossal diamond wedding ring, costing more than everything I owned in the Philippines before I met Cole, alongside the simple gold band with the ancient Baybayin script, *Pamilya,* on it. The Filipino word is for *family,* which reminds me of the family the ocean stole from me in the tragic hurricane. My grip tightens, and I stand taller.

The ocean is not taking anything else today! I am going to survive!

I grip the boat for dear life. My fingers white-knuckled with terror but holding.

This time it's different. I'm not a helpless child, and I have something to fight for. I bite my lip and widen my stance, using my elbows to protect my belly from hitting the boat with the pounding waves.

Minutes stretch into a never-ending night as I search the turbulent waters for any sign of Cole and keep my hands gripping the boat. The boat's erratic jostling and the relentless storm are making me nauseous.

The boat is like a toy thrown around in the waves, bobbing and staying afloat despite the storm. Every scream of the wind and crash of the waves erodes my hope of finding Cole and escaping the storm.

"Cole! Where are you?" I sob with rain-soaked words and a scratchy sound.

Clinging to the boat, isolated and scared, my imagination smashes me harder than the waves. With each lurching movement of the boat, I fear it'll be the last, and it'll flip or crash into something and sink.

Each second is a battle to stay afloat, to hold on, and to stay alive. The darkness of night mingles with the unrelenting storm shrouding me in black despair.

The man who promised me a family, a future, and a dream life is nowhere-*gone*! And I'm left alone, barely able to hang on in this horrible Alaskan ocean without the faintest idea of what to do.

Cole's gone, and I'm going to die, too.

I grip my only lifeline, the radio.

"Please! Someone! Help me! Please," I sob into the radio.

Chapter 2: Jackie

The storm changes the rolling ocean waves into walls of unpredictable breakers, pounding into my boat, The Sea Otter's Pride. Hours earlier than expected, the storm hit, but that's how the weather is at the end of summer in Alaska, unpredictable.

I should head back to the shore, but my clients are waiting for a boat taxi across the bay, and I'm already halfway there. My heart hammers as I contemplate my options: complete the trip for my waiting clients or be realistic, turning back to the safety of Homer as the violent storm front grows more hazardous each minute.

"Stupid weatherman," I grumble, the rain drops hitting my ball cap and the wind pulling my blonde hair from the messy bun stuffed under it as I drive directly into the gray storm.

I genuinely hate to lose the business-really the money-as I own and operate my one-woman water taxi service. The boating business is profitable in the touristy summer. Still, in the fall and winter, I can barely keep the business afloat while competing with the larger, established taxi service, the Homer Harbor Hopper.

There's enough ferrying business in Kachemak Bay for all of us if they weren't so damn competitive. I grind my teeth, thinking about their slogans, Ride with the Best or Float with the Rest, leaving our competition in our wake for over 40 years.

I tuck a strand of hair behind my ear and shake my head. My trustworthy boat is over forty, but I've only started ferrying people in the last few years. Since the Hopper only hires men and my boat is my only source of income, doing my small ferry runs is a more reliable income than fishing with its unpredictable, dwindling annual salmon numbers.

Homer's leading economy is fishing, but tourism is booming, and I pivoted despite learning a new business model. As long as I'm alone, on my boat, on the water, I'm living my dream.

Growing up in this tight-knit community, people trusted my boating skills to ferry them and their cargo across the bay. Although the Hopper has larger vessels with many scheduled trips across the bay, I can make my own hours and accommodate last-minute, unscheduled cargo and passengers. I do my best to help others, even referring passengers to the Hopper's boats when I'm overbooked, but they've never sent me a client-not a single one.

Thus, I work solo without business partners or support from the Hopper ferry captains. I overhear them radioing that they are too full to take all the passengers. In spite of knowing I can move their extra people, they avoid radioing me and make their passengers wait hours for their next trip across the bay.

Consequently, each of my clients appreciates my immediate ferry service and the personalized service I provide. I appreciate their reviews and return business. I might not have a fancy boat or ten sailings a day, but I get the job done, and I'm a damn good sailor!

The rain increases and I pull out my yellow rain jacket from the locker under my bench. If I can't complete this trip to drop off cargo and pick up passengers across the bay, the clients may switch to using the Hopper's evening ferry. I should've turned back when I saw the winds start kicking up two hours ago. Now, even if I make it across the choppy waters, I'm stuck over there since we can't return until the storm passes.

"Dammit!" I slam my hand on the wheel and sigh, relenting to the storm and turning my boat around to go to Homer. I pinch my nose and push my hair back in defeat as the wind starts howling and the sky darkens.

It's just my luck! I'm losing the fare, time, and the gas to get this far. Plus, I might lose the clients if I can't make it across later tonight.

Since visibility sucks, I mess with the buttons to set my navigation system for Homer when my radio crackles.

"Someone. . . HELP. . one!"

A desperate female's voice pierces through the radio's intermittent static with garbled pleas for help in the soupy gray evening. There's no location attached to the distress call.

I turn the knob to increase the volume, and the voice stops, eerily silent.

Scanning the dark waters with the brewing storm already causing choppy waves, I look. Without a doubt, someone is in danger out here, and without any other vessels on the water, I may be their only chance.

Surely, I can't be the only one who heard their call, I think, my heart in my throat. I nervously lick my salty lips as I continue searching the rough water. My hands tighten, gripping the wheel, my eyes narrow at the horizon beyond the frothy crests for any sign of another vessel.

The first rule of boating is that rescuing is a priority, no matter what. And the closest vessel is required by maritime law to give aid.

Without hesitation, I slow The Sea Pride's engine to help locate the distressed vessel. My boat is solid as it plows through the fierce waves. I steer it into the oncoming waves and toward Homer, hoping to see the caller in distress.

Surely, they'd be en route to Homer, not navigating the storm in the middle of the bay.

However, no other vessels are in sight, and I certainly haven't seen any Coast Guard vessels out here. If the mayday caller is here, I must find them before the storm traps them, giving them no chance of rescue until it passes.

I crack my knuckles and grip the steering wheel. A mayday from a boat in this kind of weather doesn't end well.

Suddenly, a red ship bobbing inside the storm's chaos catches my eye. The boat is battered and adrift, taking relentless blows from the ocean's fury.

My pulse quickens. This must be the Mayday call!

I see the boat taking the full force of the crashing waves into its port side, jostling the vessel and causing it to tilt brutally, unbalanced in the violent waters. The wounded vessel must be water-logged with its engine off and unable to bow into the waves for protection. My jaw tightens at the boat's situation, barely staying above the foaming sea.

I pilot the Sea Otter's Pride with the singular purpose of reaching the boat to provide assistance and rescue if needed. My reliable skiff responds readily to steering through the waves despite being pushed and pulled by the storm.

As I approach, my eyes lock onto a lone, odd, pink-clad figure without a jacket or life vest on the foredeck, starboard side.

A woman!

Her petite frame is hunched from the cold, fear, or an injury. Either way, she needs to get out of this desperate situation.

She sees me and begins frantically waving both arms in the universal distress sign, with her shouts swallowed up by the storm.

Dammit! If she doesn't hold on to the boat, I'm going to be rescuing her from the water!

"Hold on. I'm coming. Just keep holding tight," I say uselessly, as one of my hands grips my steering wheel and my other signals high above my head a nonverbal response that I am coming. The fragile woman won't be able to hear me over the roaring of the storm.

I guide my boat as close as I dare in a position alongside the tilted drunken vessel.

Quickly, I move to the side and extend my hand for her to take.

"Grab my hand!"

My boat lurches as her larger vessel slams against the side of my smaller but sturdy boat. I don't hear the boats crashing with the storm's howling winds, but I feel the jarring with each wave.

Motioning frantically for her to grab my hand before the next wave hits us, my urgency thrusts the sopping-wet woman into action.

For a moment, she hesitates, looking back into the Bay behind her. Then, her brown eyes locking onto my eyes, she lets go of the rail and reaches for me.

I'm close enough now to see her red lips trembling with her dark, wet hair in her eyes and mouth.

And then, with a quick surge of determination, she lunges toward me, her fingers grasping mine.

I lock her hand in mine, the cold seawater dripping down our intertwined fingers. With all my strength, I pull her from the unstable deck of her boat onto the relative safety of mine. The boats collide in the turbulent waves, adding a chaotic dance to her rescue.

"I'm Captain Jackie. You're going to be fine," I reassure her, my voice firm despite the situation's urgency. The wide red eyes that meet mine hold fear and gratitude. I want to wrap her in a warm blanket, shield her from the biting cold, and cocoon her in safety. But time is of the essence, and I have to move quickly. "You're safe now. I've seen worse weather." I manage a tight smile, attempting to convey confidence, but her stunning, albeit wet, appearance steals my breath, and my heart flutters unexpectedly.

Why is she alone out here? Who is this exotic beauty?

I furrow my brows and wipe the hand not holding hers over my face. I'm momentarily caught off-guard by the delicate touch of her hand and the intensity in her big brown eyes. I'm drawn to her, like a salmon swimming upstream, drawn to its innate spawning grounds. I find myself irresistibly pulled towards her amidst the Alaskan storm.

She's dressed in a way that screams I'm a tourist in the harsh Alaskan weather—bedazzled flip-flops, expensive jewelry, a summer dress now clinging to her tan skin. The tropical flower pinned in her drenched black hair adds a touch of unexpected beauty to the grim surroundings. As she stands there, her tiny frame accentuated by the soft curves visible through the soaked fabric, I can't help but imagine her fitting perfectly on my lap.

I shake that enticing image from my head. Stay focused! This is an emergency, I scold my wayward thoughts.

"Are there any other people?" I shout over the roaring wind, pulling her closer to me to hear me and to shield her from being swept away by the rough waters. The urgency intensifies, but in the midst of the storm, a different kind of intensity simmers—a magnetic pull that goes beyond the immediate danger.

Her voice whispers with a plea, "Cole. . .He's gone, he's gone..." Her unfocused eyes look into the ocean, and she continues to whisper.

Colton Sanders? I was so focused on her that I didn't recognize the Homer Harbor Hopper's logo on the yacht.

Amid the raging Alaskan storm, I find myself grappling with the irony of rescuing none other than my business rival, Colton. Figures.

"Where is he?" I holler, pulling her closer to decipher her mumbled words over the wind. Her slender form melds into my solid frame, her pale face inches from my mouth. Despite my urgent inquiries, her wide eyes, fixated on the storm outside, show no comprehension.

"Did he fall overboard?" I ask louder, giving her a gentle jostle. She nods numbly, her legs giving way, and I instinctively catch her, cradling her cold, delicate frame in my arms.

I guide her to a sitting position on the deck, securing her safety with an extra life jacket and tethering her to the boat's lifeline, a safety rope around the boat to keep her from falling overboard. Ensuring she won't be tossed overboard in the storm's chaos becomes my priority.

"How long has he been in the water? Is he wearing a life jacket?" I demand, desperate for information. She nods, eyes shutting.

"No! Stay awake with me! Tell me! What happened to Cole?" I lift her, slightly shaking her until her brown eyes flutter open.

"Where is he?" I shout, pulling her closer so she can hear me and I can try to decipher her mumbling.

"How long has he been in the water? Is he wearing a life jacket?"

She nods her head, and her eyes shut.

"No! You need to stay awake with me! Tell me! What happened to Cole?" I lift her and lightly shake her until her brown eyes open.

Cole won't survive in this Arctic water long. I have to find him NOW!

"I don't...maybe...two hours...he has a life jacket," she whispers with a cracked voice through her chattering teeth, her brown eyes brimming with tears.

I clench my jaw, my eyes softening. Maria isn't whispering in shock- she's exhausted, her voice lost from hours of yelling and searching for Cole.

"I'm Maria," she whispers, closing her tired eyes.

A pang of guilt hits me for shouting and shaking her. She's tiny, fragile, and exhausted. I can only enclose her in my arms, hug her into my warm body, and bury her against my chest. I want to comfort her and assure her that she's safe.

Cole's life is seriously in danger if he's been in the icy water for so long. Prolonged exposure to Alaskan waters, even in the summer, can lead to hypothermia. Despite his life jacket, the longer he remains in the water, the slimmer his chances of survival become. The ticking clock amplifies the urgency, leaving us on the edge of hope and despair.

I snatch the radio to call in the mayday report and toss my life ring in the water to mark the spot for the Coast Guard to search. As I convey the information, I wrap Maria in a rain jacket and put a dry winter hat on her head while keeping her propped up next to me.

"Location? Over," the Coast Guard radios back, and I look at the coordinates, relaying them.

I scan the waters once again for any sign of Cole.

"Captain, come into Homer. We've marked the location. The storm front is increasing, and the winds will be up to forty knots within the hour. Over."

I glance at Maria, wondering if she understands the significance of what the Coasties relayed to me. The storm is worse, and they want us out of it, but to leave means Cole loses any chance at rescue.

A cold wave crashes and washes us with icy water.

Not that I think he's alive. . . but leaving leaves no possibility of his survival. I swallow. We can't stay out here any longer and risk our lives in the storm.

"We are going back. The Coast Guard will take over searching for him," I tell her.

The boats are still beside each other, rocking and slamming together in unison.

"Maria, what's wrong with the boat?" I look at the expensive bayliner; it seems fine, just waterlogged.

She shrugs, her eyes still shut, and replies, "Nothing. I don't know."

I'm close enough to easily tie my towline to Cole's boat and drag it along.

I secure the larger vessel to mine because if she were my boat, I'd want someone to bring her in and not leave her to be destroyed by the weather. With the quick tow secure, I turn my attention to navigating back to the harbor, and Maria clings to me, her body trembling.

Gazing upon the stunning, delicate woman I've rescued, her eyes gently closed as she slumps against the deck, every instinct urges me to gather her into my arms, to shield her in warmth and safety. Yet, the pressing need is to remain steadfast at the helm, guiding us swiftly to the safety of the shore. The internal struggle between desire and duty intensifies, creating a yearning to cradle her fragile form despite knowing my duty to get us to shore.

With the quick tow secure, I turn my attention to navigating back to the harbor, and Maria clings to me, her body trembling.

"We can't leave him. He's my family. He's all I have," she whispers, her voice heavy.

I hold her closer and look down at her, my lips tight, unable to give her false hope. I lean in, hugging her tightly against me, watching the water, looking for him in the waves, and navigating silently to the harbor. I set her down, increasing the throttle to get us back to safety.

Amidst my driving, a muffled sob reaches my ears. Her warm, honey-brown eyes lock onto mine. The tension is heavy, yet we have a quiet understanding in our shared moment. I give her a small smile of hope, and her uncertain eyes lock onto mine with raw emotion.

She stands and wraps her arms around me, her warm breath grazing my neck. The storm rages around us, pushing and pulling at us. Our connection is the only solid, warm place to grasp. Our bodies are pressing together, and my heart races with a determination to survive and to save her.

Instinctively, I move my face closer to hers, leaning in, my mouth pressing tenderly against her salty forehead. As I pull back, her head tilts up, and her lips, soft and parted, draw me in. Her warm breath tickles my cold lips, making my stomach clench with a raw desire exploding.

Before I can taste her and wrap her into my arms to give her more, the boat lurches with a bang, throwing us hard into the steering wheel. I let go of her to yank the wheel back on course to Homer.

Something is off! The boat isn't powering into the waves but dragging backward. I look back, and the back of the Sea Otter's Pride is gone—destroyed!

The ocean quakes underneath us, making the boat tip, and the gray sea swallows us whole.

The cold water jolts me into action, and I grab her life vest, unclipping the lifeline, before she is dragged underwater with my sinking boat.

"Swim," I shout towards her wide, dazed eyes, dragging her along as we swim a few feet to the larger vessel we were towing.

My arms and legs are already numb by the time we reach the side of the boat. I grab the taut tow line coming off the boat and roll myself aboard, then reach down and hook her life vest to throw her on deck with me.

Miraculously, we made it aboard Cole's boat. Maria's dazed and barefoot but appears unharmed.

I crawl over, immediately unhooking the tow rope that was attaching it to the Sea Otter's Pride. My boat is almost invisible, sinking beneath the waves from the ripped-out tow shaft.

Damn! My boat insurance premium is going up, for sure.

There's no time to worry or do anything about that—we need to get ashore before we are killed by the storm or freeze to death.

I turn the key of the Harbor Hopper's boat, and the motor sputters, roaring to life. Thank God!

Increasing to full throttle, we bump over the waves to shore, leaving my sinking boat and Cole behind in the bay.

Chapter 3: Maria

Confident Captain Jackie, sporting her vibrant jacket and her piercing, narrowed eyes, deftly navigates us through the turbulent waters toward Homer. I let the fear and tension drain from my body, trusting that we're almost there—she'll keep me safe. After all, she's rescued me twice already.

I silently assure myself, I'm going to be okay. And the Coast Guard will rescue Cole.

Jackie's grip on the wheel is steady, her eyes fixed on the path ahead as if daring the storm to challenge her. The boat rocks, but Jackie moves with the fluidity of someone intimately connected to the ocean. Her movements are deliberate as she expertly guides us through the waves.

The dampness clings to my clothes like a second skin, but Jackie is unfazed, her yellow jacket a beacon of resilience against the storm.

A surge of gratitude washes over me for Jackie's presence. Without her, we'd be facing certain death. Relief floods my mind at seeing her appear during the perilous moment of losing Cole and trying to find the will to survive. Jackie saved me and enveloped me in her protective embrace.

The next thought is the other moment- when her gentle lips touched my forehead. My lips tingle as I contemplate what almost happened after that. . . Swiftly, I push aside that random, impulsive, and oh-so-wonderful thought.

I'm married, building a life with Cole, I remind myself. My flash of desire was just gratitude and my relief at being found.

With determination, I focus on the current task—to get back to Homer, bring Cole home, and ensure our dreams remain.

A bright light engulfs us, and I blink.

"Here they are, Lieutenant Johnson," an Asian man announces, and the Coast Guard ship emerges before us, shining a spotlight and interrupting our freezing trip and my spiraling thoughts.

Jackie's voice cuts through my confusion, "We made it, Maria!"

I shield my eyes. "Is that the Coast Guard?"

Jackie grins, her yellow jacket glowing in the light. "Yep, they're our ticket home."

As we approach the Coast Guard ship, I shiver. Jackie lays her hand on my shoulder. "You did great out there."

"Thanks," I manage to mumble, feeling exhaustion and relief.

I see the familiar backdrop of the Homer Boat Harbor behind the ship. Astonishingly, I survived two boating emergencies and arrived back home to Homer.

I look down at my bare feet. I must've lost my sandals in the panicked swim to the boat. Tears form as my mind wanders to the memory of skipping these docks in my golden sandals to enjoy a carefree day on the water with my new husband, Cole.

My missing sandals are the least of my problems.

I wipe my wet, numb cheeks on the jacket Jackie found and draped around me as the large Coast Guard Rescue ship approaches.

As they come within reach, Jackie's hand finds mine, a silent reassurance that we're in this together. She helps me to the men waiting to wrap us in blankets and take over the boat to let us ride with them into Homer.

I breathe with shaky laughter, sinking into the seat. I'm visibly shaken with exhaustion and fear. However, we've survived the storm. I slump into the arms of a Coast Guard man helping me onto the larger vessel.

Sergeant Wong, his name displayed on his uniform tag, reassures me, "You are going to be fine." He wraps another woolen blanket around my trembling form as we reach the docks.

My numbness begins to wear off, allowing the emotional turmoil of my ordeal to finally sink in. Tears stream down my cheeks, and a lump lodges itself stubbornly in my throat.

The salty scent of the sea lingers in the air, clinging to the damp clothes drying to my body. I inhale deeply, absorbing the reassuring sounds of the men organizing themselves to assist.

Despite the cold, Jackie snaps into action, securing the boat to the dock before the Coast Guard crew can tie it up. She's holding out a hand and helping them to step off the ship. I watch in awe of her skill and confidence.

Following her example, I throw my legs unsteadily over the side of the boat and reach out my trembling hand to the wooden railing on the dock. Jackie takes my arm to help me. Her gaze meets mine in silent acknowledgment of what we've survived.

I nod mutely, unable to find the words to express my gratitude and the anguish in the uncertainty of not knowing if Cole is out of the storm yet.

I turn my attention to the Coast Guard personnel as they approach me with authority.

Jackie stands beside me as the handful of uniformed men advance, their clean appearance starkly contrasting the gloomy weather. A sigh of relief escapes me, marking the transition from turmoil to relative calm. I'm ready to hand over the weight of Cole's desperate situation to the professionals who assist in such emergencies.

An older, stern-faced officer steps forward, his authoritative tone cutting through the howling wind. "I'm Lieutenant Johnson," he declares, eyes scanning us to assess our condition. "I understand you've been through quite an ordeal. Where's the man, the Captain, in charge?"

Jackie steps forward confidently, "I'm the one in charge. I called for the rescue."

He frowns looking from her to me, then looking past us. "Can you tell me what happened?" His eyes settle on Jackie since there's no man, and she's less shaken than me.

Her expression tightens, and her robust and assertive demeanor falters as she explains, "Cole, Maria's husband, fell overboard and is missing. Maria originally called for a rescue, and I was the only one out there, so I responded. Perhaps you should talk to Maria first?"

He looks at me, his brow furrowing even further, then back to Jackie, deciding to ignore me. "You said you saw someone swept overboard?" His lips pinch tightly together as he rubs the back of his neck.

I wipe my eyes on my sleeve, wondering if I appear hysterical or unhinged. I can't blame him for ignoring me—Jackie is the local boater, and she's confident and collected. In comparison, I'm barefoot, crying, wrapped in a blanket, and mute.

"I'm the captain of The Sea Otter's Pride," Jackie interjects, with her unwavering voice, "which responded and rescued Maria. My boat became disabled and sank. We came back on Cole's boat. He's the one missing, and I called in his coordinates for a rescue."

As she speaks, the Coast Guard ties up our Hopper boat behind the large rescue ship.

"When did he disappear?" Sergeant Wong asks me.

I start to answer, but Lieutenant Johnson interrupts, "Let's talk to the girl who speaks English first."

Jackie's eyes narrow at him as he ignores me. I shrink behind Jackie. I don't mind being invisible. I'm used to it, being a foreigner in this very-white town. But I need to know if they've found Cole yet.

She protests, "No. You'll want to ask Maria those questions."

"Do...You...Work," he pauses after each word, "...for Cole?" He asks me slowly and deliberately as if I can't understand basic English.

My voice barely makes a whispering whoosh as I try to respond. I've completely lost my voice. My heart speeds up, and I look at Jackie.

She sees my wide eyes and takes my hand, stepping forward to address Lt. Johnson.

"Maria isn't an immigrant fishery worker. She was boating, and her husband fell overboard."

"Where...is...the boat...you were fishing...on?" The older man continues in the same slow rhythm and louder volume.

"Do you have your work visa with you?" he presses, while Jackie tightens her grip on my hand, and I shake my head.

"Do you speak English, ma'am?" Sergeant Wong asks, his eyes showing apology.

I nod, wondering if they even sent out a search for Cole or if their assumptions about me are causing a delay in his rescue. My eyes start watering again and I wipe them on my sleeve.

Jackie stands next to me, fingers wrapped around mine in support.

At least I have someone willing to help and listen.

Johnson speaks louder and slower as if expecting me to confirm everything he's already decided, "You think around four in the afternoon he fell in illegally fishing? Did he have a work permit?"

My husband is in danger, and he's not listening to me! A frustrated sign escapes my lips, and I want to fight back, yelling and punching. My breathing increases, and I start shaking.

"You have to find Cole. What are you doing to find Cole?" I finally croak, swallowing the lump in my throat, ignoring his useless questions.

Jackie says firmly and commandingly, "Maria isn't a deckhand. She's Colton Sander's wife. He went overboard during the storm. You need to get your thumb outta your ass and find him."

Johnson's eyes fix on Jackie in a cold grey stare. As tension mounts, I look at the storm, realizing this delay in conveying the information to the US Coast Guard is costing Cole time that he might not have.

Sergeant Wong steps closer. "Cole? Homer Harbor Hopper, Captain Cole?"

I nod. My voice is shaky, but I'm determined to get Cole home. "Yes, sir. We were caught in the storm," I begin, my gaze shifting between Jackie and the man. "My husband, he fell overboard. He was there, and then. . . he disappeared. I couldn't find him, and he was wearing a life jacket. That's when Jackie came. She searched but didn't see him either. Her boat was ripped apart by my boat pulling out the back of hers. Her boat went under.

. . Everything was getting lost in the storm. Cole. He's out there. We couldn't find him. He's still out there."

My words are urgent, running over each other. I know I'm repeating myself, but I need them to listen to me and find Cole.

"Was he ferrying people?" Johnson directs the question to me, realizing the potential scale of this search and rescue operation.

"No. Today is his day off, and we were alone on the water taxi, just enjoying the water," I reply, wiping snot and tears with the blanket.

Jackie adds, "You did everything right. You called for help and searched for him until I got there."

The more likable guy, Sergeant Wong, adds, "I'm afraid it's not uncommon for storms like this to get the best of even the most experienced boat captains."

"We'll initiate a search and rescue operation immediately. But I must prepare you for the possibility that the odds of survival in these conditions are slim," Johnson says with a more sympathetic tone, knowing I'm Colton Sander's wife.

The weight of his words settles on me, a reminder of the sea's unforgiving nature. My heart aches, and my eyes water at the thought of Cole lost in this storm and the hurricane that took my family. Jackie's hand offers comfort, and she puts her arm around me as I sob.

"You think around four in the afternoon he fell in?" Johnson asks Jackie, confirming my story.

"That's what she said," Jackie responds. "The storm was sudden, and I almost didn't see her or Cole's boat until it was directly in front of me. Then my tow bar got ripped out from the stern, and the entire aft was totaled, so we got on the Hopper Boat to get back here."

"Cole's boat wasn't damaged?" Johnson scowls and drills Jackie, "Captain, you never saw her husband fall overboard?"

"It's like I said, I heard the call and found her."

"So anything could've happened to your husband? Do you want to amend your story?" Johnson looks at me with steely eyes, and I open my mouth without words.

I cross my arms in the bulky blanket to hug myself, my numb legs buckle, and I start to fall.

Jackie raises her arms to support me, growling to him, "You have the coordinates and all the information you need. We are getting a drink at the Salty Dawg. Find us there and update us on the search ASAP."

"Sounds great," Wong says, opening a map and trying to direct Johnson's attention away from scowling at me.

Continue reading Maria's heartwarming story in

Wilderness Rescue: Stormy Hearts.

at HarmonyNoble.com.

Chasing that next heart-racing, can't-put-it-down love story? Find your next escape at HarmonyNoble.com

Join the reader list for exclusive updates, new releases, and special giveaways

Welcome to the breathtaking wilderness of Alaska, where love blooms as wild and beautiful as the northern lights.

Prepare for an exhilarating journey through diverse, LGBTQ+ inclusive romances set against the backdrop of charming small towns and untamed frontier.

Immerse yourself in a series that celebrates Alaskan culture and heartfelt relationships featuring trans, lesbian, bisexual, and two-spirit characters. From gripping rescues to soul-stirring connections, these standalone sapphic tales celebrate strong women navigating love and life with grit and determination in Alaska's rugged beauty.

Explore the standalone sapphic romance stories in the Wilderness Rescue Seriesat HarmonyNoble.com

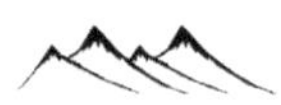

"I loved learning more about Alaska... I also loved when they finally got their happy ending, it was super satisfying."—**Reviewer on Crashing Into Love**

She took the job in Alaska's wilderness to prove herself. Instead, her journey to love is the adventure.

City nurse Riley Thompson has her future perfectly mapped out—until she's stranded in a remote village. The only bright spot? The village elder who saved her life and sees right through her polished outer image.

Mary's wisdom as a Yu'pik elder has guided her people through countless storms, but talking a drunk pilot into landing safety—and saving a beautiful city nurse in the process—might be her greatest test yet.

With Riley's career pulling her back to city life?

Will tradition and personal ambition pull their hearts in opposite directions?

Available now at HarmonyNoble.com.

"Unthaw My Heart" is a thrilling standalone novella to warm your heart and prove love reigns even in deadly conditions."

—Reviewer on Unthaw My Heart

In the harshest of winters, can a Christmas Eve storm turn two broken hearts into something beautiful?

Caught in a Christmas Eve blizzard, Dr. Makayla and Army mechanic Pauline are trapped in a remote Alaskan cabin—facing more than just the freezing cold. In the unforgiving wilderness of Alaska's Caribou Hills, survival is about opening your heart, facing your fears, and finding the strength to trust someone new.

As they navigate icy car crashes, broken promises, and the harsh realities of coming out in a town that feels too small, Paul and Mak discover that love is the one thing that can unthaw even the coldest hearts.

"This is my first Female/female romance I believed and I thought it was very cute and entertaining. The plot line was fresh and unique and I loved the characters."—**Reviewer on Winning Love**

Lights, camera, complication: Two coworkers team up to face off in Alaska's ultimate reality dating show, but when the game is love, who's really keeping score?

Stranded in Seldovia after their cruise jobs sink, Poppy and Baby join the outrageous new hit, The Smoking-Hot, Arctic Bachelor, scheming to win the cash and charm the hunky bachelor.

When prize and love collide, they flip the script, turning the romantic game show into a jaw-dropping celebration of true love.

Available now at HarmonyNoble.com.

"A Riveting Rollercoaster of Love and Life in Alaska!" **—Reviewer on Stormy Hearts**

I steer my ship into the vast sea to lose my past. Instead, I found her. Now I chart a course to search for her lost love... A course that ends in my heartbreak.

In freezing Arctic waters, Maria's world shatters when her husband vanishes overboard, lost to the icy depths of Kachemak Bay. But fearless Alaskan boat captain, Jackie, swoops in to save her from the storm's clutches.

Despite Maria's grief and the town's judgment, their bond deepens, weaving a tale of love against the odds.

As they navigate through the stormy seas of prejudice and their own hidden pasts, they must choose—risk everything for love or let fear tear them apart?

Explore each standalone sapphic romance in the Wilderness Rescue Series at HarmonyNoble.com.

"This novel is an absolute gem! The author skillfully weaves a romance that feels genuine and inclusive. Sterling and Chloe's love story is not just about love but also self-discovery and embracing life's unexpected twists..."**—Reviewer on Scoring Love**

Hockey was her game plan until love changed the rules.

In Fairbanks, where temperatures are at -66°F, a hockey star's perfectly planned life is about to get checked by love.

When hockey hotshot Sterling saves local artist, Chloe, from falling through the ice, neither expects the heat that ignites between them.

Can Sterling trade her player status for Chloe?

Will Chloe risk revealing that the coach tormenting Sterling is her ex-husband?

Available now at HarmonyNoble.com.

"I enjoyed the story a lot. . . some angst, and plenty of comic fun. I enjoy the insights into Alaskan life."**—Reviewer on Flooded Hearts**

In Alaska's wildest kitchen, a chef discovers that the best recipes can't be found in a cookbook when love is on the menu.

When uptight chef Lucy flees her toxic ex and lands in Cooper Landing, Alaska, she has one goal—becoming a Michelin-starred sensation.

Deb—beloved local farmer and keeper of indigenous traditions—believes any disaster can be fixed with wisdom and a community feast.

A flash flood threatens their tiny town, throwing these opposites together. Lucy—who doesn't do chaos or feelings—finds herself knee-deep in a rescue.
As her orderly life unravels, could messy, wholehearted Deb be exactly what she needs?

Explore each standalone sapphic romance in the Wilderness Rescue Series at HarmonyNoble.com.

"A captivating journey of love and self-discovery that will stay with you long after you've turned the last page."

Sometimes the steepest mountains lead to the sweetest collisions-a story of skiing, healing, and love.

Get ready to race down the ski slopes where two paths cross on a wild ride of love and self-discovery.

Caitlyn, affectionately known as Cat, must overcome her inner turmoil and grumpiness to reclaim her belief in herself to find love.

Peekaboo is a dedicated ski instructor with an infectious zest for life that inspires others with disabilities to embrace joy and adventure. Yet, behind her smile is a heart yearning for more.

Torn between loyalty to her devoted partner and a longing for fiery passion, will Peekaboo choose love?

Available now at HarmonyNoble.com.

"If you love opposites-attract romances that make your heart race, this is your next favorite book." **—Reviewer on Tides of Love**

Some days change your life forever. This is one of them.

Serena lives for adventure, but when a storm sweeps her into a dangerous rip tide off, she ends up stranded on a rocky outcropping, face-to-face with a cute, but unimpressed local.

Bree, a self-proclaimed Alaskan loner, wants nothing to do with the thrill-seeking surfer. But when the rising tide traps them, they'll have to rely on each other to survive.

What starts as a fight for survival turns into something much more—one storm, one day, and an undeniable connection that neither of them saw coming.

Explore each standalone sapphic romance in the Wilderness Rescue Series at HarmonyNoble.com.

"...If you are a fan of insta-love, this novella will be right up your alley. It is a cozy, sweet romance, with an exciting backdrop of the Alaskan Iditarod." **—Reviewer on Iditarod Love**

Love, survival, and the untamed Alaskan wilderness collide in the race of a lifetime.

Brace yourself for a thrilling journey on snow-swept trails of interior Alaska.

Brynn Dawson has ice in her veins and one goal—winning the Iditarod with her legendary dogsled team. But nothing prepares her for Morgan, an upbeat race volunteer with a knack for getting under her skin.

When disaster strikes during the start of the race on the crowded streets of Anchorage, their worlds collide in a daring rescue that ignites something neither of them saw coming.

"The Alaskan setting is beautifully woven into the story, offering authentic details without slowing the pace. A fun and satisfying romance." **—Reviewer on Frozen Hearts**

Trapped. A desperate escape. A frozen rescue. An unexpected love story.

Mae came to Alaska for one season and a life-changing paycheck. Instead, she finds herself with no money, no way out—and on the run.

Lost on the frozen tundra, she's rescued by Taylor, a fur-clad trapper with a guarded heart and a past she'd rather leave buried. But as danger closes in, survival draws them together, and an unexpected love begins to take hold.

In Alaska's unforgiving wilderness, escape may be impossible—and love may cost them everything.

Explore each standalone sapphic romance in the Wilderness Rescue Series at HarmonyNoble.com.

Aurora's Wilderness Love: Hot Girl Summer Love

Where the odds are good, but the goods are odd—welcome to Alaska, to discover a love more untamed than the wilderness.

Aurora knows two things for certain: dating in Alaska is a contact sport, and survival isn't just about navigating frozen tundra—it's about navigating the heart. Broke, desperate, and one dating disaster away from giving up, she's determined to rewrite her story, one hilarious misstep at a time.

With more men than women in this last-frontier dating landscape, Aurora is about to discover that finding herself might be the greatest adventure of all. Armed with nothing but her wits, a killer sense of humor, and an uncanny ability to turn romantic catastrophes into comedy gold, she's ready to prove that sometimes love finds you when you least expect it—and usually when you look absolutely ridiculous.

Get ready for a heartwarming Alaskan rom-com where hunting for love is the ultimate wilderness sport, and Aurora is determined to bag her happily ever after.

The odds are good, the stories are better!

Aurora's Wilderness Love: Just a Little Fall Crush

In Alaska, the ice is cold, but the workplace tension is scorching.

Aurora's back—and this time, she's juggling college, a corporate job she's barely qualified for, and a secret relationship with her infuriatingly poised boss. (Yes, that boss. The one with cheekbones sharp enough to slice through HR policy.)

After surviving the wilds of Alaskan dating, Aurora thought she knew chaos. But nothing prepared her for office romances, unread syllabi, and learning her absentee father might not be so absent after all. Between quarterly reports and unexpected DNA results, Aurora is forced to confront what it really means to grow up—and who gets to be called family.

With a found-family cast of coworkers, an all-too-supportive best friend, and a boss who kisses like a dream but critiques like a CEO, Aurora's once-simple survival plan turns into a rom-com of epic proportions. Can she keep her job and her heart intact—or will it all crash faster than her GPA?

Tropes you'll love: Secret workplace romance, "we shouldn't be doing this... but we are", found family in unexpected places, college girl chaos meets boss-level confidence, and a big emotional reveal with heartwarming fallout.

In a place where the moose outnumber the men, love was never going to be easy—but Aurora's about to learn that the greatest discoveries happen when you finally stop running and start showing up.

The odds are still good. The feelings? Even messier.

Aurora's Wilderness Love: Christmas Cruise Mistake

Escaping winter in Alaska? Check. Accidentally honeymooning with a stranger? Also check.

When a last-minute tropical Christmas cruise invite saves university student, Aurora, from an awkward post-break-up holiday and the freezing snow of Alaska, she packs her bikinis, her sass, and a plan to have fun and forget her epic break-up.

But a massive booking mix-up later, she's now pretending to be the runaway bride of the woman who left at the altar. *Oops!*

Desperate and ready for a second-chance, Aurora's trapped on a couple's cruise filled with love exercises. Aurora's just trying to survive awkward icebreakers, too many trust falls, and the very real sparks flying with her accidental not-wife. *The plan?* Fake it 'til they dock.

A steamy karaoke duet changes everything. Aurora's heart is reignited and the cursed cruise might be what her tender heart needs.

Tangled in lies, tequila, and tension even a conga line can't break, Aurora's about to learn that running from romance leads her straight into the arms of a woman she never knew she needed.

The odds are still good. The drama? *It's a full-blown shipwreck.*

Other Titles by MELODY BEST & HARMONY NOBLE

For the most up-to-date list visit HarmonyNoble.com

Aurora's Wilderness Love:

Hot Girl Summer Love

Just a Little Fall Crush

Christmas Cruise Mistake

Wilderness Rescue Series:

Crashing Into Love

Unthaw My Heart

Winning Love

Stormy Hearts

Scoring Love

Flooded Hearts

Healing Hearts

Tides of Love

Iditarod Love

Frozen Hearts

Trapped Heart

Tangled Love

Coffeehouse Romance Series:

Love, Joy & Lattes (Joy's Story)

Test Driving a Millionaire (Tara's Story)

Shattering Crystal a Bully Romance (Crystal's Story)

Choosing Love, Namaste (Meaghan's Story)

My Accidental Christmas Fiancé (Monica's Story)

Coffeehouse Romance Short Stories:

Joy's 4th of July Holidate

Tara's Valentine Holidate

Crystal's Easter Holidate

Meaghan's New Year Holidate

Monica's Halloween Holidate

Joy's Coffeehouse Romance

Snag the latest swoon-worthy reads and stay tuned for upcoming stories at HarmonyNoble.com.

About Author - Harmony Noble & Melody Best

Meet the unstoppable twins from the rugged wilds of Alaska, the writing duo, Harmony & Melody. Fueled by endless lattes, their character-driven stories brim with authenticity, humor, and heart—featuring Alaskan grit, journeys of self-discovery, and swoon-worthy happily-ever-afters.

When they're not crafting adventure romances, these twins can be found hiking trails with breathtaking views, enjoying charming coffee shops, or exploring new worldwide destinations together.

Join the e-newsletter for exclusive content and give-aways at website: harmonynoble.com

Email: TrueLoveWriters@gmail.com
Instagram/Facebook/TikTok: @truelovewriters

www.ingramcontent.com/pod-product-compliance
Lightning Source LLC
LaVergne TN
LVHW010654110826
845149LV00014B/3088

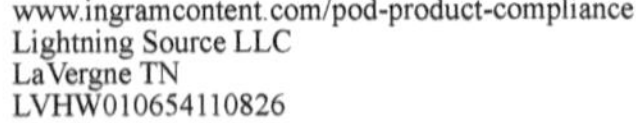

* 9 7 8 1 9 6 3 0 7 4 9 9 4 *